CHASING THE YETI

An Adventure in Snow

Jeyamohan

An English translation of *Pani Manithan*

Translated from the Tamil by

V. Shyamala

JUGGERNAUT BOOKS
C-I-128, First Floor, Sangam Vihar, Near Holi Chowk,
New Delhi 110080, India

First published by Juggernaut Books 2026
Originally published in Tamil as *Pani Manithan*
by Kizhakku Pathippagam

10 9 8 7 6 5 4 3 2 1

P-ISBN: 9789353457808
E-ISBN: 9789353459451

Typeset in Adobe Caslon Pro by R. Ajith Kumar, Noida

Printed at Thomson Press India Private Limited

This story is a glorious blend of fact and fiction. Fiction begins where fact ends. Follow the clues and find the yeti. If you manage to find the Snowman – Shhhh … keep it a secret. Don't let anybody know (except perhaps your best friend!).

Contents

1

Imagine if ten thousand huge buckets of ice cream were scooped and spread all over the ground. That was how the slopes looked.

There was knee-deep soft, white snow everywhere. Eight people were wading through it. Six were military men. The other two were their guides. They were wearing thick thermal wear, leather on the outside and lined with wool inside. On their feet were snow boots with spikes. The men had on dark sunglasses that would reduce the bright glare from the snow.

All around them, snowy peaks stood tall. They looked like mountains of sugar stacked up. The sun had set by then. But even when there is no sunlight, the glaciers remain bright for a long time. This phenomenon is known as internal reflection.

The men were in Depsang Valley. This place is 7,000 feet above sea level. It lies to the north of the Ladakh plateau. At such heights, neither plants nor animals can grow or survive. The only sound you can hear is the howl of the snowy winds.

The only sound heard there was the howl of the snowy winds. Had it been a constant sound like that of a whistle, there would have been no fear. When it rises and falls in pitch, however, it indicates that a snowstorm would follow. During a snowstorm, the snowflakes would fall like heavy rain. It would completely cover the flat plains in snow. No one could escape.

Likewise, there would also be sounds of ice slowly cracking, heard constantly throughout. This is the sound made by the glaciers freezing again and compressing when the temperature drops. Suddenly, one part of the snowy mountains would split and fall apart. Dragging along the people on it, the soil would slide down to the bottom of the mountain.

The people who live on the Ladakh plateau are of Mongolian ancestry. Their language is Ladakhi. Their religion is Buddhism. The Ladakhis know how to move around the mountains. They are trained in climbing snowy peaks. Army people would often appoint them as guides.

To the north, beyond the Depsang Valley, lies the Karakoram Pass. A 'pass' means a path between ranges of mountains. It is the gateway between India and China. In 1962, the Chinese launched an attack on Indians via this pass. This is why the Indian Army always keeps a watch over it.

The six soldiers were engaged in surveillance operations. They had to reach their army camp at the nearby peak before nightfall. Once night falls, it becomes impossible to walk on snowy mountains. One would freeze to death right there. So they walked fast.

The group's captain observed the peaks and slopes keenly through a telescope. There was no colour other than white. This is why it was difficult to identify anything on the snowy mountains.

He switched the regular lens to the polarizing lens and looked into it again. Now, the snowy plain could be seen in varying shades of blue, red and violet. When seen in different colours, even minor differences in the plains would become visible.

No danger was evident to his eyes. To the north were China's Kunlun Mountains. They looked like unmoving smoke standing still against the sky. In the north-west, the Khangchendzonga peak was visible. The evening sunlight fell on it. It seemed to turn red, as if a burning light was reflected off glass.

The Captain was about to move his eyes away from the telescope. At that moment, his sight fell on a particular thing. A deep, long impression was visible on the snow slope. It appeared to be the marks of a vehicle that had passed by. He raised his hands and gave the danger signal. Immediately, the guides stepped back. Soldiers with rifles moved forward. Unlocking the safety on their guns, they walked in single file.

They descended the slope and reached the place. The marks had begun to fade off because of the falling snow.

It was only once they neared the area that they realized those were not tyre tracks. They were in fact elliptical and stretched in a straight line. The Captain bent down and observed the marks keenly. He could not deduce what they were.

One of the guides called out something loudly. The other immediately knelt down and bowed respectfully. Both seemed really terrified.

'What are they saying?' the Captain asked.

One of the soldiers knew Ladakhi. He said, '*Sahab*, look at the marks closely. These are …'

The Captain immediately understood. 'Ahh!' he yelled.

He could not believe what he was seeing. It was the impression of a very big foot! At least three times bigger than a human footprint. When they went a little further, he found a clear footprint that had not yet faded, with even the impression of the toes intact.

If these were real, the man who made these footprints could even be two times taller than the average man. He would be taller than an elephant and a giraffe. Almost 12 feet in height!

'Those are the footprints of the Snowman. He is the sentinel of the Himalayas,' said one soldier.

'The Abominable Snowman?'

'Yes. Apparently, his footprints are often visible in this area. A few people have even seen him. The people of Ladakh revere him,' said the soldier.

Other soldiers began to tremble with fear. One soldier said, 'Sahab! Let us leave immediately.'

The Captain took photographs of the footprints from various angles using his photographic equipment.

The mountain peaks started to look like blue-coloured glass walls. This indicated that it would soon be dark. They hurriedly started climbing up the mountain and walking towards their camp.

Why Did China Start the War?

The Himalayan mountain ranges lie between India and China. China declared that some of these ranges belonged to them. India did not agree to this. Jawaharlal Nehru was the prime minister then. Mao Zedong was the Chinese premier.

So, in 1962, China launched an attack on India. China also captured many peaks that belonged to the Indian territories. Jawaharlal Nehru was a pacifist. So, we were not ready for war. The areas that China occupied then are still with it.

2

Ladakh's capital is Leh. The army headquarters for that area is situated there. Major Pandian entered his office that morning when he was informed that the Brigadier had summoned him. In Ladakh, the mist would clear only around 10 a.m. Offices would begin functioning only around 11 a.m. As it was winter, even noon looked like dawn there.

Brigadier K.K. Nair was in his office. His cabin was filled with the smoke from his cigar.

When Pandian knocked, the Brigadier called out, 'Come in'. He went in and saluted. The Brigadier offered him a seat and placed the Malayalam paper that he had been reading on the table. Pandian asked, 'Has the post arrived, Sir?'

Posts would come to Leh only once a week. Newspapers would come via post too.

'No, this is an old newspaper. I was just reading it,' said the Brigadier.

Soldiers who were in active service, having left behind their native towns, would read old letters and newspapers again and again. They found pleasure in thinking of their homes and their friends and family.

The Brigadier pulled out an envelope and placed it on the table, saying, 'Look, here is a job for you.'

Pandian opened the envelope. There were several photographs inside. They were photos of varied hues, taken using a coloured filter lens. The photos were all of the same footprints.

'These were taken by our surveillance team last week in Depsang Valley. They immediately informed the headquarters. We have received orders to conduct an inquiry and ascertain the truth behind this,' said the Brigadier.

'Seems to be the footprints of a *rakshasa*, a huge demon,' said Pandian.

'They are saying these are the footprints of the Himalayan Snowman. In the last fifty years, our soldiers have supposedly seen such footprints about thirty times. Photographs have been taken in seventeen instances. They are all in this file. Have a look!'

Saying thus, the Brigadier held out a file. Pandian opened it.

There were several photographs in that file. He noticed that these footprints had supposedly been sighted only in the north-western regions of the Himalayas.

'We have sent research teams out there many times. But, when they reach there, they find nothing conclusive. The local people there do not disclose anything. So, this time, our orders are to conduct covert investigations,' said the Brigadier.

'Are we sure this is not a conspiracy or trick by our enemies? Could it not be their intention to frighten us away from undertaking surveillance in certain areas?' asked Pandian.

'It is not that easy to reach the peaks of that particular mountain range. If these footprints have been fabricated, would not the prints of the person who created it be visible?'

'True,' agreed Pandian.

'Our scientists claim that these footprint-like marks are depressions that naturally occur on the snow. Long cracks appear often on glaciers. Soft snow settles inside the crevices. Then, the air trapped inside contracts due to the cold. Immediately, small pockets of depressions occur in a line, like how bubbles rise and burst in a marshy swamp. I personally feel that this could be the real reason,' said the Brigadier.

'Seems to be a plausible explanation,' said Pandian.

'Not just that, if such a man exists at all in that snowy region, what would he eat? There is nothing in that barren place except for snow,' said the Brigadier.

'That's true,' admitted Pandian.

'I think all this is the imagination of the Ladakhi people. Our soldiers hear such tales too when they are there and are gripped by blind fear. You must go there, investigate and submit a report. This job should take only a week, that's about it,' said the Brigadier.

Pandian looked at the photographs again. 'No, Sir! It is not that simple. Whatever you've said sounds right. But there is still one doubt that remains to be cleared.'

'What is that doubt?' asked the Brigadier.

'Look at these photographs. All the footprints are roughly the same size. If these were depressions formed naturally on the snow, why are they not of different sizes?'

'True. A valid point,' said the Brigadier.

Pandian took leave from the Brigadier. He kept thinking about those footprints. The town of Leh had slowly started to come alive. The snow-covered Himalayan ranges could be seen in the distance. Does that Abominable Snowman really live there?

Twelve feet in height?! As tall as a young palm tree! How would it feel to meet him alive? Pandian left for his office, burning with curiosity.

Mule Postmen

A postman brings the post to our homes. Sacks of letters are taken from one town to another by vehicles, usually vans or buses. But on the Himalayan slopes, the bags of letters would be loaded onto the backs of mules and sent to various places, as there would be no roads or paths for buses or other vehicles to ply. Posts would come only once a week because the mules would take at least a week to walk there from nearby towns. Mules are employed for this work as they are very strong and can climb mountains without tiring.

3

In the evening, Pandian returned to his home. It was a small house with three rooms.

In the colder regions, the walls of houses would be thick and sturdily built with heavy stones. Inside the stone walls, there would also be walls made of wood. Similarly, the roof would also have two layers. The air trapped between these two layers would reduce the cold from seeping in, to an extent. This is similar to how we wear two or more layers of clothing when it is cold. The roofs (and therefore the ceilings) of the houses would be very low and the rooms would be very small. The reason is that, when the room needs to be heated with external means, it would be easier for a smaller area to heat up quickly right?

Pandian's house had been allotted to him by the Indian Army. He had a cook, an office assistant and a maidservant too. They were employed by the army too. He was ranked as a 'Major' in the Military Intelligence. This is a senior rank and position.

Pandian, a thirty-year-old man, was 6 feet tall and dark-skinned. While he was well built and had a strong body, he was not married. His parents lived in his native village of Chinnamangalam in the Madurai district of Tamil Nadu.

Pandian changed his clothes and went to his room. He wiped his face with a towel dipped in hot water. People who live in the cold regions do not bathe every day. One does not sweat there, so there is very little chance of the body getting dirty.

After making sure the electric heater was fully turned up, Pandian sat down. He started going through the files and notes very carefully. Then, he took out two sheets of paper. In one he wrote: 'The Snowman Does Not Exist'. He listed down the supporting causes for this in bullet points. In another sheet of paper, he wrote: 'The Snowman Exists'. He listed out another set of supporting arguments under it. For an hour, he kept contemplating and writing. This method is very useful in helping one think clearly. Clarity can be obtained in any confusing issue if one is able to write it down thus.

He was able to write down eighteen reasons under 'The Snowman Does Not Exist'. He could write down only one reason under 'The Snowman Exists' – the supposed footprints. They seemed to be real prints made by a huge foot, after all.

He took out another sheet of paper. On it he wrote: 'The Footprint Was Formed Naturally on Snow'. He thought up four reasons for it and jotted them down. In another paper he wrote: 'The Footprints Were Fabricated by Enemies'. He then listed down six reasons for that. There was only one reason for the depressions to be that of an actual snowman. It was that the impression was really big.

Pandian thought hard. Why couldn't a human footprint be that big? Perhaps he could have worn really big shoes. The mark on the soft snow could have expanded and grown bigger when the snow melted.

It is very important that the investigation began at the right place. If one begins investigations with a false premise, it will lead to a waste of time and effort. *How can an ordinary human footprint become three times bigger? Investigating this would be the right place to start*, he thought.

Satisfied with his idea, he got up and made a trip to the bathroom. On his way back, he wondered whether he had closed the tap properly. So, he turned back. It was then that he noticed the wet marks left by his footwear.

Immediately, an idea struck him. He picked up one of the photographs and looked at it intently. There were marked differences between those big footprints on the snow and Pandian's footprints. His footprints were in a straight line. But those marks on snow were pointed outwards, and were quite a distance apart. That is, the prints apparently made by such big feet were slightly rounded on the edges. If the man who made these were to stand with his feet together, the footprint would resemble a 'U'.

Pandian then picked up a coloured chalk and drew footprints similar to that of the snowman's on the floor. Then he tried to put his feet into those outlines and walk. At first, he had to lift each leg and walk with difficulty. Then, he realized one thing. He tried to walk with legs slightly bent. He also tried to walk with hip bent. Then it became easier to walk on those prints.

This could signify that the man was probably not able to stand fully erect. His legs might be short too. His feet would be turned outwards. It seemed like he walked swaying from side to side.

Which animal would walk like that? Normally bears walked on all fours. When it walks on two legs, its back would not bend. Could it be a monkey? Yes. Gorillas walk with such a gait. Pandian wet his feet again. He walked the way gorillas do, swaying his hands, with feet spread apart.

The marks made on the floor by his feet were exactly like those made by that Snowman! If so, the Snowman is a monkey! A twelve-foot-tall monkey! How does it live on the snowy mountain range? What does it eat there? Why has it not entered any neighbouring village even once?

Pandian immediately wrote a letter to the Army's Military Intelligence. In that, he requested information to be gathered about the following and sent to him.

> All information about monkeys needed immediately. Need to meet a research expert on monkeys. Need to meet a research expert on Kashmir and the Himalayan geological formations.

After sending the letter by special post, he began making preparations for his journey. The winters in Kashmir are bitterly cold. Our region (Tamil Nadu)'s temperature would be around 30° Celsius. When it falls to even 20° Celsius, we claim that it is very cold and snuggle in a blanket. When the temperature is 0° Celsius, water freezes and becomes ice. Temperatures in Kashmir could fall below that, even going to –22° Celsius.

During such times, nobody would dare to climb up the snowy mountains. It would be difficult to come back alive. But Pandian was very daring. He had more than his share of courage. Moreover, he had already received several kinds of training. Even when faced with hardships, Pandian would perform his duty.

Kargil War and Military Investigations

The Indian Army has two divisions – Combat Arms (those who fight) and Services (those who support). The Infantry, Armoured Corps and Artillery are part of Combat Arms and often engage in face-to-face combat. The Corps of Engineers comes under Services and is responsible for constructing bridges and roads. The Corps of Signals is also a part of Services and is responsible for operating radio and telephones. When it is difficult to attack with huge forces, small groups of specially trained soldiers are deployed. They are called Special Forces. This is how the commandos were successful in surprising the enemy at odd hours. The Military Intelligence was formed to spy on the enemies.

4

Two weeks later, Pandian received a post from the Military Intelligence Centre. It had all of the details he had requested.

The information about monkeys was of no use to him. Only small-sized monkeys were found in the region, that too only in the foothills of the Himalayas. Monkeys cannot live on snowy mountain peaks, as they are adapted to live in warm climes. Moreover, there were no big-sized monkey species to be found in India. Chimpanzees, gorillas and orangutans are the 'bigger monkeys'. They live in Africa, and some islands in Indonesia including Java and Sumatra.

Pandian was disappointed. There was no chance that the footprint found on that snowy peak was that of a monkey. If not, whose footprint could it be?

The notes also had information about one Dr Divakar. He researches people living in the Himalayan regions. It was mentioned in the report that if Pandian could meet the doctor, he could obtain further information.

Pandian set off to meet Dr Divakar. The name of the mountain village where the doctor lived was Ta-Ping. It was 200 km away. He travelled by jeep and reached the nearest army camp. After that, he had to climb up a steep mountain, which could be done only on mule-back. The next day, three mules were brought in. They belonged to and had been raised by the Indian Army.

A mule is the offspring of a female horse and a male donkey. It is as tall as a horse but its face is like that of a donkey. At the same time, mules are far stronger than a donkey or a horse. They easily lift even very heavy loads on their backs. They can climb up even steep slopes and do not get tired easily.

The soil in the Himalayan regions is not very stable or concentrated. The soil's consistency would be like that of the soil thrown out when a well is dug. It is ferrous in nature (red) and has calcified stones. When it rains the ground would become as sludgy as a field. The soil at the peak of the mountain would often slide and fall down.

Only mules would know how to walk carefully on that soil. They would ascertain the depth of the slush just using their sense of smell. Their hooves are wide and hence their legs would not slip.

Pandian sat astride a mule. His gear was loaded on another mule. His guide climbed atop the third mule. He belonged to a local mountain tribe. Without their help, no one would be able to travel on those mountains.

On that mountain slope, even though it was late morning, the light was low, as if it had just dawned. Snowy peaks stretched as far as the eyes could see. The peaks of the mountain were covered by a blanket of white snow. There was only the red ferrous soil on the mountain slopes. In some places, small meadows of green grass could be seen; the sheep grazed there. The tribal people who herded them sat there in groups. They were smoking long pipes made of clay, stuffed with tobacco. They played sweet music on small wooden pipes.

That mountain slope was dotted with several tiny villages in which the mountain tribes lived. They crossed many such villages. While they were crossing one such village, they heard the sound of bells and hurried over to watch. They saw ten villagers walking, carrying a cot. They were wearing clothes made of black wool. A young boy was lying on that cot. He appeared to be around ten years old.

Pandian was already well versed in the tribal dialect. Hence, he was able to talk to one young tribal man who stood there, grazing his flock of sheep.

'Has he died?' Pandian asked.

'No, he is a demon's child. So they are going to throw him out of the village,' said the tribal lad.

'Why do they consider him to be a demon's child?' asked Pandian.

'Last week a group of herders from our village went to Ta-Ling to graze sheep. They lost their way and went really far up the snowy mountains. This boy and his father were also a part of that group. He suddenly caught a fever and could not walk at all. So, they left him at the peak of the mountain. The others somehow managed to find the right route and returned. Twenty days later, this boy came back.'

'Alone?' asked Pandian.

'Yes. Today morning, when we came out of our homes, we saw him. He was sleeping on the warm ashes from a coal stove. How could a young boy make his way back like this if not for the help of the demons?'

'It really is astonishing,' said Pandian.

'The demons will follow him and enter our village. That is why they are going to sacrifice him to the mountain goddesses,' said the lad.

'Let us follow them,' said Pandian to the guide.

'No! It is dangerous!' The guide was frightened.

'We have to save this boy. There is some mystery here. We have to find out what it is,' Pandian said stubbornly.

The Himalayan Mountain Range Was Once an Ocean

Approximately 40 million years back, South America and Africa were part of the same landmass and were of the same continent. It was known as Gondwanaland. India was also a part of Gondwanaland. Asia and Europe were one landmass.

Over a period of time, even as Earth cooled and its top crust dried up, its hot and fluid mantle moved the solid plates of Earth's crust and separated it into various parts. The Indian landmass got separated and dashed into the continent of Asia. Due to the pressure, the land bent, rose high and became a range of mountains – this is the Himalayas. The ocean shifted away from there.

What is currently the Himalayan region was under the ocean a long time ago. Even today, in many of the Himalayan peaks, fossils of fishes and other sea creatures can be found. This is the reason why even today, the soil in the Himalayan regions is soft and rich in calcium content. In contrast, the soil in the southern part of India is made from hard, black rocks. Even today, the mountains of the Himalayas are increasing in height steadily. This is the reason for the frequent earthquakes that occur in this region.

5

Pandian and the guide unobtrusively followed the men who were carrying the boy. They stopped when they reached a small mound. Pandian climbed on it and observed what was happening.

There was a huge cave beyond the mound. At its entrance, there was a big rock slab, almost like a cot. There was a small stone plinth near it. The people who had been carrying the boy put him on the big rock. A man who appeared to be a priest climbed up on the small plinth. He held a stout staff in his hand.

The priest shouted loudly, 'Oh Goddesses of the Mountains!'

Immediately a resounding echo was heard from an opposite peak. Then another echo was heard from another peak. Echoes kept resounding from each and every peak.

The guide got frightened. He cried, 'The Goddesses of the mountains are speaking! I am afraid! I am leaving,' and tried to run away.

'Stay!' ordered Pandian angrily. The guide stopped.

The priest shouted, 'Shall I sacrifice him?'

The mountains replied with resounding echoes. They all fell down to their knees and prayed. Then, without looking back, they quickly walked away.

'Only bones would remain on that rock tomorrow morning. The Mountain Goddesses would have eaten him up,' the guide said, trembling with fear.

Once they all had left, Pandian said, 'Come, let us save the boy.'

'No! That would be dangerous. The Mountain Goddesses would eat us up too!' cried the guide.

'It is not the Goddesses that eat the bodies. Look up at the sky. You will understand,' said Pandian, pointing up.

Tiny black dots could be seen dotting the sky. Gradually, they grew bigger, and the duo could see that they were mountain eagles. They were really huge birds and they kept flying closer.

Petrified, the guide sat down with his head in his hands. 'Mountain eagles!' he wailed.

'Yes. They live in hollows on the slopes of the mountains. They come as soon as an offering is placed upon this rock,' said Pandian.

The guide said, 'They are deadlier than the demons of the mountains. If they do not get their prey, they would devour us and even the mules.'

Pandian pulled out his gun.

'There are hundreds of eagles. How many of them can you shoot down? There is no place even to run and hide in this open meadow,' moaned the guide.

The number of eagles on the sky swelled. Some of them dipped and soared like smaller airplanes. The mules brayed anxiously and jumped in fright.

'There's a way,' said Pandian. He ran and climbed onto the stone pedestal. His hunch proved to be right. The cave was like the mouth of a loudspeaker. Whatever sound he might make while standing on that rock would be amplified manifold. It would ricochet on the mountains and echoes would be heard repeatedly.

Pandian shot into the air with his pistol. The gunshot noise was amplified and rose to the sky. A few moments later, loud gunshots were heard from the opposite peak. Then the same sounds were heard from another peak. Like thunder, the sounds kept resonating.

The frightened eagles scattered and flew away. 'Wak! Wak!' they shrieked, deafeningly loud. Losing their focus and direction, they scattered and flew off. Pandian lifted the boy and came running. The mules stood stricken by fear. He placed the boy down on a mule and strapped him up securely with a belt. The mule shivered and kicked its legs. Pandian scratched between its ears and patted its back. It calmed down.

They left that place hastily. Soon, it grew dark. Temperatures dipped and extreme cold set in. The boy's body was very hot. It was obvious that he had a high fever. It was difficult to find their path in the darkness. Pandian looked up at the sky. He knew how to find the cardinal directions with the help of stars. But right then there were no stars in the sky.

'Do you know the way?' Pandian asked the guide.

'It has become dark,' said the guide hesitantly.

Nothing was visible in the pitch-black darkness. In a little while, it would become bitterly cold. They could die of cold then. They did not know what to do. Then, a wind blew in from the west.

The guide said, 'Ah! I got the way!'

'How?' asked Pandian.

'Follow me,' said the guide and walked ahead.

Gradually, Pandian began to understand. The scent of incense wafted in from somewhere in the west. It was based on that the guide had found the right direction!

Following the scent of incense, they walked ahead. They noticed the glow of flames in the distance. 'That is the village of Ta-Ping,' informed the guide.

In most mountain villages, there is a large pit in the centre of the village. They would fill it with firewood, light a fire and keep it burning throughout the night. Their cows and goats would be tied up around that fire pit, and would be kept warm by that fire. Such a fire would prevent wolves and other such animals from attacking and snatching away the cows and goats. People who had lost their way could see the flames from a distance and find their way back.

Only when they came near did Pandian realize how big a fire it was! They had piled logs of wood and set them alight. The flames leaped high, approximately as high as a man!

As they neared the village, the fragrance of incense grew stronger. The entire village was enveloped by it. It was then that Pandian understood the reason for the scent. The burning logs were from the deodar cedar tree! It is from this tree that regular incense is often extracted. It is a really valuable wood. And here, they were using it as firewood!

'Are they burning deodar wood?' asked Pandian, astonished.

'What else can they do? There are no other big trees in the forests here!' said the guide.

They reached the entrance of the village.

One Sound, Many Echoes

In a castle called Woodstock in England, a sound made at one place would echo seventeen times. In Czechoslovakia (now Czech Republic and Slovakia), in a rocky place near Adlersberg, a sound would echo seven times. These are popular tourist spots. How does this happen?

When our voice falls on a hard surface and ricochets back to our ears, we hear an echo. If that sound falls on one solid surface and from there it ricochets off to another solid surface, two echoes would be heard. Similarly, if it falls on three such surfaces, three echoes would be heard and so on.

6

The villagers had built a wall made of big rocks stacked above each other, surrounding the village. There was only one entrance. It was closed by a big wooden door.

On seeing the flames, the mules ran ahead. They crashed against the wooden door and brayed. Immediately, many mules that were inside began to bray too. Yaks and sheep also lent their voices to this chorus.

Some people could be seen lighting the lamps inside. Two people came holding hurricane lanterns in their hands. 'Who is that?' they queried.

Pandian stepped forward and showed his identity card. 'I am Pandian. I have come to meet Dr Divakar,' he said.

They took his card, held it near the lamp and examined it closely. At last, one of the other men inside said, 'Alright, let them in.'

Pandian and the mules entered the village through the open gateway. It was then that Pandian noticed two more people standing in the shadows. In their hands, they held modern rifles. They escorted him to

Dr Divakar's home. When they knocked at his door, the doctor, carrying a lamp, opened it.

Dr Divakar looked to be fifty years old. His face was round, smooth and clean-shaven. He was wearing thick-framed spectacles.

'Who are you?' asked the doctor.

Pandian produced his ID card and the letter from the Military Intelligence.

The doctor went through them. 'Come inside,' he said.

'This young boy is unwell, Doctor,' said Pandian.

'What happened?'

Pandian briefly narrated all that had happened.

'Bring him in and lay him down on the table,' said the doctor.

There was a bamboo cot inside the house. Pandian laid the boy down on it. The villagers took the guide with them. The doctor examined the boy and said, 'I think it is pneumonia, but the fever has subsided. I can see his body has begun to sweat. So, he will recover soon.'

Pandian opened his leather shoulder bag and took out a fresh set of clothes. He changed into them and sat down. The villagers offered him a clay bowl of hot porridge. It was made of oats flour mixed with goat's milk. It was very hot and tasty. He felt stronger after having it.

'Let us sleep,' said the doctor.

Pandian took out his sleeping bag, which was made of high-quality nylon and layered with wool inside. He slid inside and lay down, stretching his legs. He pulled up the zip and covered himself up to his neck. It felt cosy against the cold.

'How could this boy have come down from the snowy mountains all by himself?' asked Pandian.

'Several such incidents have happened before. It is believed that the Snowman saves the people lost in the snow,' said the doctor.

'Is that true?' asked Pandian.

'Yes! Several children have turned up so far. But the Snowman supposedly saves only the children.'

'If that is so, why did these villagers believe that a demon had brought him back?'

'They do not know much about the Snowman. It is only in this village and the neighbouring one that they believe so,' explained the doctor.

'Has anyone seen the Snowman?' asked Pandian.

'Only the children have seen him. But they are not able to describe him in detail. The adults have seen only the footprints. In this region, in the last twenty years, such footprints have been found one hundred seventeen times,' said the doctor.

'Oh, my!' exclaimed Pandian.

'I have collated and recorded the evidence. I have been staying here for the last six years,' said the doctor.

'Why?' inquired Pandian.

'For research purposes.'

'What kind of research?'

'I will explain tomorrow. Let us sleep now,' the doctor said, yawning.

Pandian fell asleep too.

When he woke up the next morning, the first thing he did was observe that house. Normally, houses are square or rectangular shaped. But that house seemed to be circular and dome-like in shape – like the inside of a huge clay pot. The colour was also red like fired clay. Pandian stepped out of the house. All the houses in that village seemed to be shaped like huge upside-down pots.

One villager directed Pandian to use the public restroom to brush his teeth. The village's common washroom was towards the east. Pandian noticed the doctor standing there. The doctor wished him a good morning on seeing him.

'This is a really peculiar village,' observed Pandian.

'When I first arrived here, this too was like the other villages. They had built houses made of stones. In the Himalayan region, minor earthquakes and tremors occur frequently. Gales keep blasting at high speeds. It was common for houses to crash down and kill people. That is why I have designed the houses in this manner,' the doctor said.

'How do you build these?' asked Pandian.

'These houses are built just using clay. We shape and press the clay, and make small pots out of it. Then, we dry the pots, stack them like bricks and build houses ...

like this,' the doctor said, and drew a picture in the mud with a stick lying nearby.

'Then?' asked Pandian.

'We do not construct the roofs separately. We build curved walls and make the roof with it. Then we mix the clay as a paste and apply it to the walls. It would appear as if a really huge clay pot has been inverted upside down. Then, we pile a lot of firewood inside the house and light it. The house becomes hot and the clay would harden and turn reddish-brown,' said the doctor.

'The way clay pots are baked in a kiln, right?' asked Pandian.

'Right… These houses are actually just enormous pots. The smaller pots inside the walls have empty spaces inside them. Hence the cold from outside does not enter inside. This is a lightweight house. So, even if it breaks and falls down, there would not be much damage and people would not get hurt. The entire structure is technically a single piece of clay. So, it will not break easily. As it is round in shape, it will not break even under a strong gale,' said Dr Divakar.

'It is amazing,' Pandian said.

'Let us go to my laboratory after breakfast. I will explain in detail about my research,' said the doctor.

Clay Is Enough. Cement Is Not Needed.

Dr Laurie Baker was from Britain. He was an architect, and admired Gandhiji greatly. Hence, he came to India and became an Indian citizen. He settled in Thiruvananthapuram (previously Trivandrum), where he died in 2007. High-grade clay and limestone are available in India. These are enough to construct strong buildings. It was his opinion that Europeans invented cement, as they needed a material that would set quickly and would also work under water. Laurie proved that cheaper and stronger houses could be built using just clay.

The Kerala government appointed him as the head of an organization called Nirmithi Kendra (an organization to disseminate information on low-cost building technologies and materials). He constructed multi-storied buildings using just clay. The Indian government honoured him by bestowing him with the Padma Shri.

7

After brushing their teeth, the doctor and Pandian went to the community dining hall. In that village, people did not cook in separate kitchens. They cooked and ate together. Even the yaks and sheep of the village belonged to everybody.

Their breakfast was sheep milk and barley-bread cooked over an open fire. It was really tasty. There were about a hundred villagers. Among them were nineteen children.

'How did they get rifles?' asked Pandian.

'It is given by the Army. The Army also gives them free clothes and medicines. These people are the protectors of our borders, right? Without their help, no one can traverse these mountain regions,' said Dr Divakar.

After finishing their meal, they went to the doctor's laboratory. There were several maps and photographs there. There were many books too. Pandian picked up and looked through a stack of photographs. All of them were of the Snowman's footprints.

'Till now, these footprints are the only solid evidence that we have got,' said the doctor.

'These are monkey's footprints, right?' asked Pandian.

'How do you say so?' asked the doctor.

'The feet are turned outside. I deduced based on that,' said Pandian.

'You are almost right. All the children who have seen the Snowman say that he did, indeed, walk like a monkey. Do you know the reason for that?' asked the doctor.

'No idea,' said Pandian.

'There are two reasons. Observe the footprints closely. What can you observe?' asked the doctor.

Pandian could not discern anything.

'There is an arch in the middle of a human's feet. It is because of that arch that he is able to grip the floor and stand erect, and place his foot forward and walk. But these footprints do not seem to have such an arch. They are flat,' pointed out the doctor.

'Oh, yes,' Pandian observed, surprised. He had not noticed it before.

'This is one of the most unique features of a human being. That is the reason why, among all the living creatures, it is only mankind who can walk upright,' said the doctor.

'Does this Snowman not walk then?' asked Pandian.

'He can walk. But only when his legs are spread out wide. That is why he walks with his feet turned outwards.'

'Alright, what is the other reason?'

The doctor picked up a photograph and showed it to him. It was of a chimpanzee. 'Look at its legs. Its thighs are longer. Its shin bone is shorter. That is, its legs are like two parentheses. Look, like this ...' The doctor then emphasized his point with a drawing.

'Yes,' said Pandian.

'This is the reason why its feet are turned out. It appears that the Snowman's legs too are turned like this. That could be the reason why he sways while walking.'

'If that is so, what I deduced was correct. So, the Snowman is a monkey man,' said Pandian.

'No, there is one more evidence,' said the doctor. He took out a white plate from the table. It was curved in shape.

Pandian did not comprehend what it was. He touched it. It had a smooth surface. It appeared to be a broken piece from a large ceramic cup.

'This is a bone. Part of a skull. I dug this up from under the snow mountain just last year,' said the doctor.

'What can we deduce from this?' asked Pandian.

'We can undertake research on the evolution of human species using skulls. It is known as phrenology. Based on this section of the skull, we can interpolate and draw the whole skull. Look here,' said the doctor and showed a drawing.

In that picture, he had drawn the side view of the part of the skull in red. He had completed the picture of the remaining skull in blue. In this way, he had created a complete picture of the skull. Pandian looked at it in amazement.

The doctor picked up another drawing. 'Look at this. This is the skull of a chimpanzee. What difference can you find between these two?' he asked.

'Its jaw is more elongated. The Snowman's jaw is similar to that of a human,' said Pandian.

'You are right. What other differences do you observe?' asked the doctor.

'I am not able to find any other difference,' said Pandian.

'Note the forehead. The chimpanzee's forehead is flat. But a human's forehead is large and rounded above his eye sockets. This Snowman's forehead is also like that,' said the doctor.

'Yes,' agreed Pandian.

'What can be gleaned from all this? The Snowman's brain is bigger than that of a chimpanzee. Moreover, his forebrain is well developed. So, he can speak to a certain extent. He would also have the power of reasoning and thinking. So, this Snowman is surely not a monkey,' said the doctor.

Surprised, Pandian asked, 'If that is so, is this creature a man?'

'That is what we have to find out,' said the doctor.

'Why are you researching about all this?' asked Pandian.

'What I want to know is about myself. Who am I? A human! But how did human beings come into existence? How did he get to look the way he does today? How did he become so intelligent? These are my questions,' said the doctor.

'What is the link between these questions and the Snowman?' asked Pandian.

'Though I am investigating and researching about the Snowman, in reality, it is about humans that I am researching,' said Dr Divakar.

What Kind of Animal Is Man?

How do we understand living things? First, we understand the characteristic features of living beings. Then, we see what the common feature among them is. Based on those common features, we classify those living creatures into genus and species.

Who started this method? It was the Greek philosopher Aristotle. Carl Linnaeus, a Swedish scientist built upon Aristotle's grouping idea. As per this classification, humans fall under the group 'mammals' – living beings who give birth to and suckle their young ones. As he eats both plants and animals, he is an 'omnivore'. Based on his body type, he would be classified as an 'ape'.

Physiology experts classify humans as *Homo sapiens*. All the humans on this planet belong to this *Homo sapiens* species only.

8

'You are researching mankind itself?!' Pandian asked in amazement.

'Yes,' replied the doctor.

'What is there to research about humans?'

'There is plenty. We have classified all the living things on this Earth. What species does the tiger belong to?' asked the doctor.

'Cat species.'

'Then, what species does man belong to?' asked the doctor again.

'Monkey species,' said Pandian thoughtfully.

'But there is no monkey that can count till five. However, man has invented computers. He has gone to the moon. How did this divergence occur? How did man alone acquire such immense intelligence which is not found in other monkeys?'

Pandian could not answer.

'There are several disciplines including anthropology, zoology, archaeology and psychology that seeks the answers to this question today. I, too, am searching for the answer to this question,' said the doctor.

Just then terrible howling sounds could be heard. There were also the sounds of people screaming and running. Pandian and the doctor too ran outside. The villagers were running around holding staffs and guns. Dogs howled.

'What? What?' asked the doctor.

'A pack of wolves is approaching,' said a villager.

'Where?'

'On the eastern slopes,' the villager said, running past them.

'Come, let us go and have a look,' said the doctor.

Both of them walked down the slope. Some villagers herded their cows and goats, which had gone to graze, safely back into the village. They locked the doors.

'Where are the wolves?' asked Pandian.

They had reached the slopes by then. The wolves were not there either.

'The wolves are very far off. We need to walk a long distance ahead to see them,' said the doctor.

'Then how did the villagers come to know that wolves are approaching?' asked Pandian.

'There is a small bird species called *deen* in these parts. When they notice the wolves approaching, they fly to the humans and let them know about it. If the deen scatter and swoop over our heads, it signals that the wolves are on their way here,' said Dr Divakar.

'How would we know from which direction the wolves are approaching?' asked Pandian.

'After attracting the attention of the humans, the deen signal the direction too.'

By then, they had crossed the slopes.

Far ahead, down the slope, the villagers could be seen moving in a group. The dogs too ran beside them. Small birds could be seen fluttering above their heads.

'The wolves live down in the valley. Sometimes a pack can have even five hundred wolves. They would gather occasionally, form a large group, attack the village and snatch away all the cows and goats. If they attack during the night, nothing can be done. They are very dangerous. They do not fear anything. They are skilled at unifying and attacking as a pack,' said the doctor.

'Where are these people going?' asked Pandian.

'To stop the approach of the wolves on their way instead of allowing them near the village. Come let me show you.' He led the way.

After walking a long way, the dogs stopped suddenly. Pulling their ears back, they tucked their tails under their bellies. Raising their snouts, they sniffed the air. Then, howling, they turned and ran back. Crossing the doctor and Pandian, they bounded away towards the village.

'The dogs become frightened the moment they smell the wolves,' said the doctor.

When they walked further, they could see a pack of wolves approaching the foot of the mountain. They looked as tiny as a line of red ants.

The villagers stood on the mountain. Seven or eight people went near a big boulder. The boulder had split from the mountain and stood a bit apart. The villagers placed something in the crack and crammed it inside.

'It is dynamite,' explained the doctor.

Pandian looked at the doctor in confusion.

'Keep watching,' said the doctor.

Once the gunpowder was lodged inside, all men except one stood back.

The wolves that were down in the valley had picked up the scent of humans. They stood as a group, with their snouts raised and sniffing the air. The man standing near the rock shot at the crevice in the rock with his gun. The dynamite burst with an alarming intensity. The rock split down the crack and exploded. It rolled down the slope of the mountain, gathering momentum. Big rocks rolled down the mountain like a waterfall.

The rocks fell on the wolves without respite. Many got crushed and died. Some wolves escaped and ran away. Their howls and cries could be heard faintly. The villagers hugged each other laughing.

Then, they walked back.

'Why do the deen betray the wolves? Did you spare a thought for that?' asked the doctor, facing Pandian.

'Yes. Some birds in the forest do behave like this. Once, I was travelling through a jungle. A parrot looked at me and squeaked several times. Growing suspicious, I ran and climbed a tree. Suddenly, I noticed a tiger stalking me from behind. Thankfully, I escaped.'

'Why did that bird help you?' asked the doctor.

'I do not know,' said Pandian.

'There is a link between what we discussed earlier and this. To understand better, you need to know about the Theory of Evolution,' said the doctor.

A Rhinoceros as Big as an Elephant

S.C. Jayakaran is a geologist from Tamil Nadu. He was researching the soil on the banks of a river called Karumeniyar in a place called Sathankulam, in the Tirunelveli district of Tamil Nadu. He found a large bone buried under the loamy surface.

Do you know who the half-a-metre-long skull bone belonged to? It was that of a rhinoceros that had lived 30,000 to 40,000 ago! This bone is kept in the 'geography' section of the Chennai Museum.

9

Pandian and the doctor returned to the village. There, they heard the whimpering of dogs.

A dog had retreated and was sitting near the doctor's home. Its nose was pointed towards the ground, ears were pressed against its head; it was shivering. With eyes piteously downcast, it was moaning softly.

The doctor gently scratched that dog's neck. Dogs love it if someone scratches them on their necks. The dog wagged its tail.

'Dogs greatly fear wolves. Even the dog that does not fear the lion and the tiger is afraid of the wolf. If sundried wolf excrement is kept in the pocket of one's shirt, dogs would run away, howling in fear,' said the doctor.

They both went inside the house and sat down. The villagers gathered outside and sat laughing and chatting. A man fetched a drink for the doctor and Pandian. The drink looked like *rasam*.

'What drink is this?' asked Pandian.

'It is a soup made using the bark of a tree here. It is good for health,' said the doctor.

Then the doctor gave an injection to the boy.

'Why are deen enemies of wolves?' asked Pandian.

'Those birds live eating the fleas and ticks on the bodies of the mountain sheep. When cows and sheep graze, these birds come in droves and sit on them. If sheep are devoured by the wolves, they would lose their food!' said the doctor.

'Do they really think all this before behaving the way they do?'

'They do not even have the ability to think. They have been dependent on mountain goats and sheep for a great many years. This information has, therefore, permeated their brains. Without anybody teaching them, all the deen know this intuitively.'

'Every life form has the innate intelligence and body type necessary for its survival. Dogs have a keen sense of smell. Eagles' eyesight is sharp,' said Pandian.

'This is known as adaptation. Charles Darwin discussed how, through natural selection, populations of living organisms gradually evolve. Physical and behavioural traits that improve survival and reproduction become more common over generations. This process forms the basis of Darwin's theory of evolution by natural selection,' said the doctor.

'Has anyone proved this?' asked Pandian.

'People have undertaken research on living beings that have a very short lifespan. A living thing's body adapts to its habitat, right?'

When the doctor asked this, Pandian nodded. Then the doctor continued, 'The fishes that live in the sea among the coral reefs would also look like corals. Their skin would be shiny like corals. Scientists put them in parts of the sea filled with black rocks. Each successive time the eggs hatched, the colour of the new baby fishes kept changing. After several generations, those fishes turned the colour of ash!'

'Astonishing!' said Pandian.

'This process of evolution happens even in humans. But humans have a longer lifespan. Hence, it would take thousands of years for the adaptive changes to be noticeable. Four hundred million years ago, many different species of monkeys populated Earth. The living conditions of some of these monkeys changed. When the coldness of the planet reduced, the hair on their bodies reduced too. The number of trees decreased. So, they began to walk on the ground. That is why, gradually, their backs became straighter. They started eating softer foods. Hence, their jaws became smaller. Gradually, they transformed into humans,' said the doctor.

'Yes ... This is Darwin's Theory of Evolution,' agreed Pandian.

'While the monkeys were gradually evolving into humans, monkey men lived. Some monkeys adapted slowly, while some monkeys' bodies changed quickly. For others, their brain grew rapidly. The monkey-men who evolved rapidly defeated the others who adapted slowly. When human beings evolved, they defeated the monkey men and killed them. This is how the human species spread around the world. Gradually, monkey men became extinct and disappeared,' said the doctor.

'Are monkey men not found anywhere?' asked Pandian.

'Till now, no one has ever found a living monkey man. But in the course of paleontological research, several bones of monkey men have been found. Based on that, researchers have arrived at a conjecture of how the monkey men would have looked. They have drawn pictures. When their brains were analysed, it was found that some of the monkey men were moderately intelligent. But the existence of a monkey man who was able to think like a human has not yet been proved. In anthropology, this is termed as the "missing link",' the doctor explained.

'Would this Snowman be that missing link?' asked Pandian.

'Perhaps. But, till date no evidence has been found supporting this claim,' said the doctor.

Suddenly, the boy woke up. He looked at them and screamed, 'Monkey Man! Monkey Man! He is catching me!'

How Does the Chicken Know?

Dutch scientist Niko Tinbergen and Austrian scientist Konrad Lorenz performed an experiment. They made a cardboard cut-out of a hawk. The moment a chick hatched out of an egg, they made the shadow of the cardboard hawk fall on it.

The chick got frightened and ran to hide. How did the chick know that the hawk was dangerous? The chick did not get frightened when other shadows were shown though. The reason for this is adaptation. The important things needed for the survival of a species are already embedded in the brain. They get passed down through generations.

If something slippery slithers on our legs, we immediately assume it is a snake and get frightened, right?

10

The doctor and Pandian grabbed the boy. The young boy screamed as if he had had a nightmare. The doctor sprinkled some water on his face.

The boy became somewhat lucid. Looking at them in fear, he asked, 'Who are you?'

'You are safe,' assured Pandian.

'Where is the monkey man?' asked the boy. His body trembled.

'He brought you here and left you behind. I saved you,' said Pandian.

The doctor instructed someone to bring barley soup for the boy. After drinking the soup, the boy became normal.

'What is your name?' asked the doctor.

'Kim-Tsung,' said the boy.

'Kim, why did you go to those snowy mountains?'

'I went to graze the goats. My father had come along too. I caught a fever there, and I could not walk. So they left me there. It was very cold. After everyone had left, I lay there alone. I could feel someone watching over me.'

'Who was that?' There was anticipation in Pandian's voice.

'I didn't know who. But I felt like someone was watching me. Then night fell. But, because of the snow, it was still bright. Then I saw a huge monkey standing opposite me on a glacier.'

'Monkey?' asked Pandian immediately.

'Yes. It was surely a monkey. I was afraid and cried out in fear. That monkey came ambling towards me.'

'What colour was it?' asked the doctor.

'It was the colour of ash. Its body was covered with long fur. It came near me and sang.'

'Sang?' they both said in surprise.

'Yes. A song. I screamed in fear. It lifted me up from the ground. It was a huge monkey – as tall as the trees. I sat in its palms. Carrying me, it leaped over the crevasses.'

'What did you do then?' asked Pandian.

'My father always said that wherever we go, we have to observe the peaks keenly. Only then we can find our way back. I was marking the peaks as we went.'

'Can you show the way to that place?' asked the doctor.

'Yes, I can.'

'What happened after that?' asked Pandian.

'Behind a big mountain, there was a huge snowy plain. Beyond that, there was a mountain pass. That monkey leaped across it. Beyond that, there were two big mountains. They were like some kind of entrance.

The monkey took me through them. Immediately, I felt my chest constrict and fainted. Then I came to my senses just now.'

'Wait,' said the doctor. He rushed to his lab and brought a big book. There were eight pictures in it. The first picture was that of a monkey man. The eighth one was that of a normal human. Between these, there were pictures of six types of monkey men.

'Kim, look at the monkey men in this picture. Out of these, what did the one you saw look like?' asked the doctor.

'It was not like any of these,' said Kim. He looked keenly at the pictures. Then, pointing at the second picture he said, 'It was nearly like this, but its hands were much longer. Its legs were shorter.'

Pandian looked at the pictures. The image was labelled '*Homo erectus*'.

'Alright Kim. You sleep now. Once you recover, we can go to that snow mountain peak and meet the monkey man there,' said the doctor.

Kim nodded.

The doctor and Pandian went back to the laboratory again.

'What are these?' asked Pandian, pointing at the pictures.

'These are the types of monkey men discovered around the world. Each one is at a different stage of evolution,' said the doctor.

'Who discovered them?'

'Scientists are deducing the places where the monkey-men – whose development lies between the stages of monkey and men – could possibly have lived. They excavate at those sites. It was Dr Eugène Dubois who first discovered the thigh bone of a monkey man.'

'Where?' asked Pandian.

'In the Java island. That thigh bone was shorter than that of a human, but bigger than that of a monkey. He inferred from the thigh bone that the monkey man would have walked erect. He named it as "*Pithecanthropus erectus*". It means "erect monkey man",' said the doctor.

'Then?' asked Pandian, unable to control his enthusiasm.

'After that, several skeletons of monkey men were discovered. Among these, the skeleton discovered in 1948 in a place called Neanderthal in Germany was similar to human skeleton. At the same time, it was similar to that of a monkey too. It was observed that this monkey man walked upright too,' the doctor said.

'How can that be known?'

'There is an opening in the skull where the spine enters. For animals that walk on four legs, it would be at the back of the skull. But for beings like humans, who walk on two legs, the opening would be at the straight bottom of the skull. In the skull of this monkey man, the opening for the spine was at the bottom. Its brain was big too; the frontal brain was developed. Hence, scientists named it as Neanderthal man. This monkey man is the closest to humans. It is believed that he was the progenitor of the human race,' said the doctor.

'But Kim showed us the one in the stage before it, right?' asked Pandian.

'That is what confuses me.'

'Meanwhile, this Snowman thinks, sings songs and even helps humans,' said Pandian.

'The only way to clear this up is to go and see for ourselves,' said the doctor.

Bat's Teeth

In 1912, a European scientist toured China. There, in an apothecary, some teeth labelled as 'bat's teeth' were for sale. They were big molar teeth.

The scientist bought them and sent them to European researchers. Based on it, the researchers sketched an image of the creature from whom those teeth had come. It supposedly belonged to a monkey man! Later, near the city of Peking, its skeleton was found. It had a protruding forehead and bent legs. It was about 5 feet to 5 feet 6 inches tall. It was named 'Chinese monkey man' or 'Sinanthropus'. It is also a species of monkey man.

11

From the next day, the doctor and Pandian began making preparations for the travel. First, the direction of their travel had to be decided. The doctor identified that area in a map in detail. He marked the mountains, peaks and valleys.

Then he marked the locations where the footprints of the Snowman had been discovered. He pointed out the direction those footprints had taken using arrow marks. Among them, the footprints that had been discovered before noon had been marked in red colour. The ones found after noon were marked in green.

'What can you gather from this?' asked the doctor.

Pandian observed it keenly. He understood. Laughing, he said, 'Aha!'

'What did you observe?' asked the doctor.

'All the footprints found before noon are leading away from this location. The ones found in the evening move towards this location,' said Pandian.

'What does that mean?' the doctor prompted.

'This is the place where the Snowman lives. He starts out in the morning from this place. Then he returns in the evening.'

'You deduced right,' said the doctor.

'What kind of a place is this?' asked Pandian.

'According to the land contour maps, this is just a snowy expanse. The snow never melts here. The reason being that throughout the year, the temperature remains below minus twenty degrees Celsius,' said the doctor.

'There is nothing other than snow here, right?' asked Pandian.

'Yes ... Based on images taken from aircrafts, only a snowy plain is visible. Men have never set foot there,' said the doctor.

'How can they live there?'

'That is the mystery. Let us go there in person and find out. Till now, even I was not able to go out there, as I could not find anyone to accompany me. But now you are there,' said the doctor.

Mules could not be taken for this travel. They would die in the cold. Hence, the doctor had designed and built a vehicle himself. It was made of light aluminium. It had small, thin wheels. Aluminium is a lightweight metal. But it is strong. It can be pulled along easily. They packed the necessary things in it.

Kim had recovered. Almost immediately, he began to do chores around the village. He would easily carry large pails of water from the bottom of the mountain. He would carry stacks of deodar logs too. Pandian was astonished. He asked the doctor about it.

'The mountain people are very strong. Even while climbing long distances on steep mountains, they do not run out of breath.'

'How?' Pandian's astonishment could not be controlled.

'They follow Buddhism. They revere the Tibetan *lama*s. They receive training in the monasteries from a very young age. They are knowledgeable on several kinds of yogic practices.'

The next day, they took their leave and began their journey. They climbed up the slope of the mountain. Gradually, the mud disappeared. Later, only rough, brown rocks could be seen; these had been cracked open by the cold.

As they kept climbing, the cold increased. The wind blew stronger.

'Let us climb after taking some rest,' said the doctor.

Kim sat on the ground in *padmasana*, the lotus position. With shoulders thrown out, chest expanded, he pulled in his belly. He inhaled very deeply and exhaled swiftly. He did this several times evenly.

'What are you doing?' asked Pandian.

'This is called yogic breathing. My father taught me this. I have been practising this from my childhood.'

Pandian was amazed. He did not expect that the people who lived on these snowy mountain slopes would have the knowledge and training in yoga.

'It is getting late,' the doctor said and got up.

He opened his toolkit. He took out a pipe from inside and fixed it into the ground; it looked like a small beaker with a wide neck. He put something that looked like gunpowder into it. Then he put a spike into the pipe and secured it. At the tip of the spike was tied a thin rope which was then wound around a cylinder. Swiftly, he pulled at the rod connected with the pipe. Immediately, the pipe burst like a pistol. The iron spike flew out like a bullet being discharged. The doctor had aimed the spike at a flat rock. With tremendous sound, the spike pierced the rock. The rope tied to it had also got pulled along. The cylinder spun fast, and the rope hung down from it. The doctor tugged at the rope.

'Shall we start climbing?' asked Pandian.

'Wait … The rope is strong. The spike has pierced deeply too. But still, I have my doubts,' said the doctor.

'What do you doubt?' asked Pandian.

'On the way here, I kept observing the rocks. There are very few rocks that do not have cracks. Kim, you climb up first! You weigh less.'

Kim immediately leapt onto the rope. He swiftly clambered up using the rope. A mild cracking noise was then heard. Kim immediately looked up, holding the rocky surface with one hand. Nothing was visible.

So, he climbed up again. But the cracking sound was louder now.

'KIM!' Pandian yelled.

But Kim did not show any hint of fear. Letting go of the rope, he had grabbed the rough, uneven surface of the rock and stuck to it like a lizard. Above his head, the big rock that the iron spike had pierced split open with a loud noise. Then it slowly slid down.

Pandian's heart thudded. That rock split open completely. But it did not touch Kim, and instead fell beyond where he had stuck to the rocky cliff. The rock shattered and crumbled into big pieces with a thunderous noise, and fell towards the foot of the mountain.

Once the dust settled, Pandian looked up. Kim was hanging still. 'Plucky kid,' said Pandian.

Kim clambered up the rock by clutching at the crevices between them. It looked like a lizard climbing up a tree.

When the rock shattered and fell down, the iron spike had fallen out too. It lay on the ground with the rope. The doctor picked it up. In the meantime, Kim had climbed atop the rock. The doctor threw him the rope with the spike. Kim caught it and pulled the rope up. He then tied it to a rock that was some way away from the slope. Pandian climbed up, holding onto the rope. From below, the doctor tied up their packages one by one to the rope. Pandian pulled them up. They pulled up the vehicle too. The doctor climbed up at last.

The top of the rock was a large, flat plateau. Everywhere the eyes could see, white snow lay spread over it.

What Does 'Himalaya' Mean?

How did the Himalayas get their name? 'Himalaya' comes from the compound of Sanskrit words – *hima*, meaning snow or frost and Alaya, meaning abode or home. So, 'himalaya' means abode of snow. The Himalayas are also called *himagiri*. The Sanskrit word *himam* was translated into Tamil as *imayam*.

'Himam' means 'frozen snow' and himagiri means 'mountain of frozen snow'. In India, snow is found only in the Himalayas. It is not as cold elsewhere in India.

12

Bitter cold set in, but the wind had stopped blowing. The cold even crept in through the woollen clothes. It felt like needles were being pierced into the skin.

The doctor fetched the special thermal wear from the vehicle. The three of them wore them. These clothes were specially made. Their first layer was made of thick wool. Over that was a layer or cover made by silicone sheeting. Inside that cover, thin, delicate copper wires were tightly woven together. A layer of foam rubber covered this. Finally, all of this was covered by high-quality waterproof polymer.

The front portion of that dress had a heating pad. It could be heated through electricity, and the stored heat would spread throughout the dress through the copper wires attached to it. The silicone sheet got heated up and kept the woollen layer warm. As there is foam rubber in the outer layer, the heat would not be dissipated even in the cold. The dress could be warm even up to a week.

There was a battery in the doctor's vehicle. They connected their thermal wear to it, and the dresses got heated up. All three of them warmed up. The doctor took the snow boots from the vehicle, and the three of them wore those shoes. They then wore rubber gloves on their hands. They also wore earmuffs to protect their ears from the cold.

The doctor took out a pole, used as a support while walking on the snow, and a snow axe. He handed one of each of these items to the other two. As the snow is very white, there is a chance that the glare would affect their eyes. Hence, they wore black snow-goggles too. Then, the doctor removed the wheels from the vehicle. Immediately, it became a sled. It could now slide on the snow. Pushing the vehicle, they began to walk.

'The snow is very slippery. Be careful,' warned the doctor.

'Is the snow here not crystalline?' Pandian asked.

'This kind of snow is called sleet, and it is one of the most slippery ones. The moment we put our foot on it, it will melt. That water would make us slip and fall,' the doctor explained.

'Yes. That's true,' admitted Pandian. For every foot he put forward, he felt as if someone was pulling his leg down.

'The glassy-looking snow is strong. It would be like a rock. It would not be that slippery,' said the doctor.

That snowy expanse extended quite far. As it was a completely flat plain, it appeared to be less farther than it actually was. They walked on the snow, lifting their legs high for each step.

By the time they reached the other side, the sunlight had begun to dim. Snow-covered mountains were visible in the west. Beyond them, the sky had begun turning red. Pandian wondered what the time was and looked at his watch. It was eight on the dot. But the watch was ticking fine.

'Doctor, my watch is running wrong. What is the time now?' Pandian asked.

'Eight o' clock,' said the doctor.

'Is it eight in the night?' Wonder laced Pandian's question.

'Yes. It is long past sunset.'

'If so, how is there so much light?' asked Pandian with unabashed astonishment.

'A snowy expanse is like a giant mirror. It reflects the light from the sun,' said the doctor.

Kim kept silently looking at the snowy expanse. Pandian tried to engage him in conversation. 'What, Kim? You have been coming along quite silently. Are you frightened?'

'Frightened? Why? Is the snowy peak not Lord Buddha's heart? My father would say that coming here is a great blessing.'

'Why do they call it the Buddha's heart?' asked Pandian.

'Because everything here is pure. When the earth is truly pure, it becomes like the sky. There is no sound here. This place is as peaceful as the heart of the meditating Buddha,' said Kim.

'Who told you all this?' Pandian asked.

'The *bhikshu* in our monastery taught us this.'

Gradually the sun's light turned redder. The mountain peaks visible in the distance also acquired a red hue. On all sides, only the colour red was visible in various shades. The sky was red. The snowy expanse was red. It felt as if they were standing on a huge meadow made of fire.

'The Buddha is smiling,' said Kim.

Pandian got goosebumps on hearing that. He had never seen such a magnificent sight. He even wondered whether it was a dream!

The red hue thickened. Then slowly it became dark. The light dimmed and faded across the snowy expanse the way light dims when a fluorescent lamp is put out. But some remnant of the light still remained, like how it would in a fluorescent lamp after it is switched off. Gradually, that light faded out too.

'Lord Buddha is sleeping,' said Kim serenely.

'There is no other way but to stay here. Get the tent,' said the doctor.

Pandian unpacked the tent.

'The sky is clear today. There are no clouds. We may even see the moon,' the doctor said.

Frozen Snow Everywhere

In the polar regions, snow can be found as frozen ice everywhere. Once in a while, there would be a good amount of sunshine too. Even so, the snow does not melt. Why?

When light falls on an object, light energy gets converted into heat energy and the object becomes hot. When light falls on the dust in the atmosphere, the air becomes hot.

When slanting light falls on an object, the resultant heat is lesser; it cannot melt snow easily.

Only when straight rays fall would the frozen snow melt. When snow melts thus to some extent, it becomes vapour and rises up.

In the polar regions, the atmosphere is clean. Also, it is very cold throughout. Due to this, the water vapour that had risen immediately turns to snow and falls again.

13

Pandian began to set up the tent. It was not an ordinary tent. It was specially made for snowy terrains. First, he hammered an iron peg hard into the ice. Then he spread out the tent material; it was made of high-quality polythene. There was a pump in its corner. He pumped air into it the way one pumps air into a cycle tyre. Gradually, the tent material filled with air and expanded. It became a tent shaped like a coconut shell. There was just enough space for three people to sleep, huddled close together. Pandian tied it tightly to the peg. Else, it might get blown away.

The doctor took out the food from the container. It was a roti replete with fat, proteins and carbohydrates. It was very dry and would not get spoiled for a very long time. The doctor then broke off a piece of snow and put it into a bowl. He had a small box-like equipment with him. He opened it and put the bowl inside, and then connected the box to the battery. It was a battery-operated stove. The snow began to melt and started heating up. In the snowy areas, in the bitter cold, it is not possible to heat anything over an open fire.

When the water boiled, he transferred it directly to the water bottles without exposing it to the cold. Those water bottles were encased with a heavy cork. They looked like flasks. The water had to be kept in it so it would not freeze. If it was kept open for long, the water would freeze. Sipping the water slowly, they ate the roti.

The doctor took out a small windmill whose fan blades were disconnected. He connected them and fixed them on a rod.

'What is this?' asked Kim.

'Our battery will lose charge fast. A dynamo is attached to this windmill. At night, when the windmill rotates, the dynamo will be activated. That would generate electricity. Our battery would store that electricity,' replied the doctor.

He fitted wires to the windmill. The wind was slow.

'There isn't enough wind, is there?' asked Pandian.

'In the Himalayas, winds blow suddenly, without warning ...'

'Alright ... Shall we sleep?' Pandian asked, lying down. He was very exhausted.

'Wait' said the doctor. 'Look there!' He pointed in a direction.

All three of them sat up. Pandian looked in the direction he pointed. It was the west. At first, a mountain's peak was faintly visible. Gradually, the light became brighter and the edges of the mountain became clearer, like a silver outline. It looked like a sickle's sharp edge reflecting the light.

Then, the entire mountain began to shine, gleaming bright as if molten silver had been poured over it. Immediately, Pandian realized that he too was surrounded by white light. The snow plain seemed like a sea of silver. A full moon rose in the sky. He had never seen such a huge moon. It seemed twice as big as the one he had seen from the plains, closer to the sea level. He felt as if he was flying among the stars.

Only later did he realize why it seemed to be so. The glacier reflected the sky like a huge mirror. Stars and moon could be seen on Earth too! Two moons! Unmoving! Floating!

Kim sat in padmasana and chanted:

Buddham saranam gachami!
Sangam saranam gachami!
Dharmam saranam gachami!

Pandian joined him too. As they chanted the Buddha's name again and again, their hearts grew mellow. Love for everybody in this world unfurled in his heart.

'Lord Buddha! How beautiful is this sky! How beautiful is the earth too! What a glorious life has humankind been blessed with! But because of his selfishness, man troubles others. That is the reason why he, too, is troubled. Lord Buddha, you taught great compassion to humans. Let that benevolence fill my heart too! I should not hate anyone. Bless me!' Pandian prayed in his heart.

Then, the reflection of the moon on the snowy glacier looked like a white-hued lotus. The moon in the sky seemed to be like the Buddha's footprints.

Tears flowed down Pandian's cheeks. Kim chanted the Buddha's name again. Then he bowed thrice.

'Let us go to sleep. We have a long journey ahead of us tomorrow, right?'

When the doctor said so, both of them crept into the tent and lay down.

Snowy Places and Clear Skies

Why is the atmosphere so clean in snowy areas? In the snowy areas, temperature drops to over –20° Celsius. That is why all the moisture in the air turns to ice and falls to the earth. The dust falls down along with that. But this lasts only for a couple of days. Then, moisture laden clouds gather above those places. Due to the cold, the water falls on the ground as ice, and it looks like strewn cotton balls. This is called snow.

14

The next day, it was Kim who woke up first. He had been sent to a Buddhist monastery for education since a very young age. There, he always had to wake up at dawn. No matter how bitter the cold. Due to this ingrained habit, even if he wanted to, he was not able to sleep late.

On waking up, Kim heated up half a cup of water. He washed his face with it. Brushed his teeth too. He sat on the floor, closed his eyes and meditated for half an hour.

Meditation is the act of closing our eyes and keenly observing the thoughts that run through our mind. When we contemplate, gradually, our thoughts become organized. Our heart will also attain a deep sense of peace. This has to be continuously practised for days. There are different types of meditation techniques in the Buddhist tradition. Monks teach them to children from a very young age. Children who practice them have better memory and more patience too.

Buddham saranam gachami! Sangam saranam gachami! Dharmam saranam gachami!

Kim chanted thrice.

Then, he got up and came out. There was good light outside. In the east, the sun was visible beyond the clouds. Rays of light fell on the snow in straight lines, and the glacier reflected them like a mirror.

Kim looked at the windmill. It was whirling very fast. Immediately, he looked towards the west. He could not see the mountains there at all. It was as if a very big, black curtain hung there. Such black clouds! Immediately, Kim entered the tent. He shook the doctor awake. 'Doctor Saab! Doctor Saab!' he said.

The doctor woke up. 'What happened, Kim? Why are you so harried?'

'A snowstorm is coming.'

'Where?' the doctor asked and immediately sprang up.

Pandian, too, bolted up and asked, 'Where?'

The three of them rushed out. The doctor keenly observed the western direction.

Pandian said, 'The sun is shining so bright!' He did not understand anything.

'Look to the west,' said the doctor.

'Dark clouds,' said Pandian.

'Be it in the oceans, deserts or snowy expanses, if the sky turns black, it signals a storm.'

'Let us go,' said Kim.

Pandian let out the air from the tent. It shrank with a hiss. They packed up their things and put them on the vehicle. The doctor dismantled the windmill. He looked at the dynamo. It was completely charged. He understood that there had been very strong winds during the night.

Kim began to walk towards the west.

'Is the storm not coming in from there? Why should we go towards that direction?' asked Pandian.

'There are no big rocks this side. When there is a snowstorm, we should take shelter against some big rock. If not, the cold snow would fall over us and bury us,' explained the doctor.

The three of them walked very fast. They spotted a rock at a distance. It was a high glacier. Pandian said, 'Come, let us take shelter beneath it.'

'No, it is made of just snow. It could break in a storm,' said the doctor.

'How do you know that?' Pandian asked.

'It is light blue in colour. That is because light is able to penetrate it like glass. Moreover, look at its shape. It is sloping on one side. The other side is perpendicular. This kind of ice is formed when the snow brought by forceful air gets deposited in one place. The direction from which the wind blows would be sloping and the other side would be straight,' said the doctor.

They crossed that place. Only several snowy mountains were visible around them. At last, they found a rock covered by snow but pale yellow in colour. Both of its sides were sloping. The doctor pointed at it.

'This is the one we are searching for. There is a real rock inside this. As light is not able to penetrate it, it is pale yellow in colour,' said the doctor.

They settled themselves on the eastern side of that rock. By that time, the bank of black clouds from the west had come much closer.

'Set up the tent quickly,' said the doctor.

Pandian opened the tent and started pumping it with air. Kim hammered in the iron peg.

'You have to hammer the peg in really deep. The storm is very strong,' the doctor said.

Kim hammered in another peg.

The tent was ready. By then, the darkness had come quite close to them. Kim tied the ropes holding the tent together, and the doctor tied the vehicle tightly to the peg. They both crawled into the tent.

Before entering the tent, Pandian gazed towards the west. The whole expanse of the sky in the west was pitch black. There were very frequent flashes of lightning that streaked and faded. The entire scene looked like a black wall was being cracked as it came near them.

'Pandian, come inside,' ordered the doctor. Pandian crawled inside.

There was a sound as if a huge burst of rain was nearing them. Deafening howls were heard, too. And then there was the noise that sounded as if huge rocks were splitting and imploding. The storm descended on them. They could hear the sound of huge blocks of snow lashing on the western side of the rock, below which they had taken shelter. Darkness spread everywhere.

Lightning flashed brightly through the darkness. The sounds of thunder echoed again and again. In the flashes of lightning, the drifting snowflakes shone bright. Once, when lightning struck, Pandian saw a glacier split open. In the next flash of lightning, the glacier itself was not visible.

The storm kept gaining force. Had they been standing out in the open, they would have been squashed to a pulp. Each block of snow was bigger than them. Thunder echoed in the sky and they could hear the sound of snow blocks hitting the earth – it had a particular cadence. Like the sky and Earth had come together as a percussion instrument!

Suddenly, Pandian's fear subsided. He felt that it would be okay even to die after witnessing such a scene. His excitement grew. He began to sing in a loud voice.

> The resounding rhythm of the exploding universe –
> In the void, the elements shriek in gleeful bloodlust,
> Joined by the Damaru's beat of annihilation
> And there in its midst you dance – Kali, Chamundi,
> Kankali!

Mother Oh Mother, you made me seek
Your dance of destiny!*

The doctor noticed Pandian singing. But he could not hear anything, as the resounding noise of the storm was much louder than that!

Why Do Snowstorms Occur?

Why do snowstorms occur often in the Himalayan Mountain ranges? It suddenly becomes bitterly cold in a certain area. And all the moisture in the air there becomes snow. Then the atmospheric pressure in that place dips and becomes very low. Immediately, the air from the place with a higher pressure blows there with full force. That is the reason snowstorms occur. This kind of a drop in the atmospheric temperature occurs very fast. The wind also picks up the snow that is already on the ground and whips it into the air. That is why snowstorms also blow very fast.

* Raleigh Rajan, 'Bharathi, the Fire வெடிபடும் பாரதியின் ஊழிக் கூத்து, Vedipadum', *YouTube*, 13 May 2020, https://www.youtube.com/watch?v=Nhed_ZDINOg, accessed on 3 February 2026. Composition credits: Rajan Somasundaram; translation copyright: Remitha Satheesh.

15

Gradually, the storm began to subside. The glaciers stopped breaking. The noise made by the raging wind changed. Instead of screaming and shrieking, it was now howling.

'Is this the sound made by the swirling winds of the storm?' Pandian asked, surprised.

'Yes. What song were you singing earlier?' asked the doctor.

'It is a song by Bharathiyar. He is a great poet in our language,' said Pandian.

'I have heard about him,' said the doctor, whose mother tongue was Hindi.

When a flash of lightning lit the area, Pandian witnessed a scene in front of him. There was a huge pillar in front of him that looked to be linking the sky and Earth. That pillar was moving.

Pandian understood that the wind had gathered the snowflakes and was moving them along like this. That pillar moved away, and then stopped. It was broad at the base, and that broad base moved gradually upwards. Towards the tip of the pillar, it spun like a wheel. Spinning thus, it reached the sky and disappeared.

'That whirlwind has moved upwards,' said the doctor.

Then, in the place where the wind had whirled, it appeared as if it were raining. The snowflakes that had risen upwards now poured towards the Earth. When there was another flash of lightning, a mound of snow could be seen in that place.

'A new glacier is born,' said the doctor.

Pandian looked at Kim and asked, 'Were you frightened?'

'What is there to fear?' asked Kim.

'Did your Buddha get angry just now?' teased Pandian.

'The Buddha does not know anger,' said Kim.

'If that is the case, what was it that happened here just now?'

'Lord Buddha's grace,' Kim said calmly.

Everyone came out.

The tent was covered with hard snow. Pandian immediately understood why the tent was shaped like a hemisphere. Had it been of any other shape, the tent would have broken easily when so much snow fell on it. The spherical shape is not easily broken.

The clouds parted and gave way to the sun's rays. They fell on the glacier. How would it look if a lamp was kept in a room with mirrors? The scene unfolding before them was like that. In all four directions, glaciers lit up. Every glacier was like an electric bulb.

'The blessings of the Buddha!' said Kim, reverentially.

The clouds scattered. The sky was visible through that. Sunlight brightened. In the west, over the peaks of the snowy mountains, a rainbow gradually became visible. Then, its colours became clearer. It then curved over and became a complete circle. Once, when Pandian had travelled in an aeroplane, he had seen a round rainbow like this.

'We are on a mountain. We are at the same height as the rainbow. That is why it appears to be circular in shape,' the doctor explained.

Pandian asked Kim, 'What do you call this rainbow?'

'This is the Buddha's *dharmachakra*,' said Kim.

'Is the Buddha everything to you?' Pandian asked.

'There is no place in which the Buddha is not present. We can find the Buddha both in beautiful things and in dangerous things. Our bhikshus would often say so,' said Kim.

'Let us move fast,' said the doctor.

They continued on their journey.

On seeing a particular peak, Kim pointed it out to them. 'See that mountain! I was near it. It was there I saw the Snowman for the first time.'

They walked towards that mountain.

'There … See in that direction. It was in that way the Snowman carried me,' said Kim.

They retraced their steps.

All along the path, icy rocks were lying about, split and broken. They crossed the cracks. It was then that the doctor stopped. He bent down and looked at something on the ground. It was a white-coloured broken part of a slate.

It looked as if it were a broken piece of a porcelain dish. The doctor picked it up carefully. Suddenly, Pandian understood! It was a part of a human skull.

'Look closely. Other fragments of this skull can be found too,' said the doctor.

They began to pick up the pieces. Many fragments were found. They even found a lower jawbone with teeth. Pandian deduced that it was the skull of an ancestor of the snowman than the one they were looking for. The reason was that it was very big.

What Is the Temperature Under the Surface of the Earth?

Earth's crust does not conduct heat or cold. At a particular depth, the temperature does not change. In the city of Paris, at a research centre, a scientist called Mossy, under Antoine Lavoisier's supervision, constructed a thermometer. This is located 28 feet under the ground, in an underground room. It is now almost two hundred years since this was built. Till today, the reading shown by this thermometer has not changed at all. It still shows 11.42° Celsius.

16

The doctor spread out all the skull fragments. Carefully, he began to put them together. He had glue in his hands, and he stuck them together using it. It had to be done really carefully. It was not easy to find the right piece of bone fragment.

At last, the skull was pieced together. It was a foot in length, and 1.5 feet in height.

'Such a big head!' exclaimed Pandian.

'He is even taller than what we estimated,' said the doctor.

'Where are the bones of his body?' asked Pandian.

'Perhaps he got buried under the ground a very long time ago. His body had decayed. Only his head had got stuck inside the rock. Perhaps his bones could be found on that mountain.'

'What can be done with this skull?' Pandian asked.

'The skull is like a big book. We can get a lot of information from it. Craniologists pour in molten rubber into the skull and let it dry. Then, when they remove the fragments, it would look like a replica of that living being's brain. They then compare that brain with that of a human and conduct their research,' the doctor said.

'What can we do in this snowy mountain?' Pandian asked ruefully.

'Wait. I am getting an idea!' Saying this, the doctor took out an ice axe from his bag. It was a sharp axe that could cut through ice. He cut out a square slab of ice from the glacier below his feet. Inside that pit, there was soft snow, as soft as ice cream. 'Soft snow can always be found under hard ice. Below that, clear water can be found.'

'Why?' asked Pandian.

'Ice is at zero degree Celsius. This layer of ice acts as an insulator. Extreme cold cannot penetrate the layer of ice. That is why the water below it would be at a temperature higher than zero,' the doctor explained.

'If that is true, is there water beneath our feet?' asked Pandian in astonishment.

'Definitely. If we dig about 10 feet into the ice, there will be good warm water. Did you not notice how even the snowy plain that we just walked across was? It was probably a lake. The water froze and became a glacier,' the doctor said.

Pandian turned and observed the path they had travelled on. 'This expanse is a frozen lake!' he muttered to himself, surprised.

The doctor scooped up the soft snow and filled it into the skull. Once it was completely filled, he set it aside for a while.

In the bitter cold, it froze and became hard ice. The doctor then separated the places where the ice had stuck to the skull fragments. After gently pulling them out, he re-attached them. Now the shape of the snowman's ancestor's brain was modelled in front of them with ice. It appeared like a real brain! The doctor observed it keenly.

'What are you able to observe?' asked Pandian.

'I do not know much about brains. I will tell you what I know. Generally, it is the back side of the brain that controls involuntary actions like breath and heart rate. The folds in the brain show one's intelligence. It is the front portion of the brain that has areas linked to speech and higher cognitive ability,' said the doctor.

Pandian observed the mould of the brain keenly. 'The front part of the brain is very well developed. There are many folds too,' he said.

'Yes. This is what I deduced earlier. The brain of this ancestor of the snowman is as developed as that of a human. He has as much ability to think as we do. He can speak. He can retain things in his memory. That is, he is as intelligent as us.'

'It is amazing!' said Pandian.

'At the same time, there is one other important thing. Look here,' said the doctor.

He pointed to an indentation in the front part of the brain. It was like the fold in a cloth. 'This is the area that controls speech. It is only in humans that it would be developed to such an extent. Similarly, in a human brain, the indentations below this are very important. It is this area that controls the functioning of our hands. In a human's brain, this would be very well-developed. The major area of our forebrain would be filled with such indentations,' said the doctor.

'But, in the snowman's ancestor's brain, this area has not developed and remains hollow?' Pandian asked.

'This is the most important thing. We have to ponder deeply on this. Language and speech skills of this ancestor of the snowman are highly developed. But his hands have not achieved dexterity,' said the Doctor.

'That is, this ancestor of the snowman can speak very well. He can think too. But he would not be able to use his hands as expertly as we do, right?' asked Pandian.

'Yes. People who are aware of human history would never believe this,' said the doctor.

'Why do you say so?'

'In the brain, the area that controls the language and the part that controls the hands are next to each other. Did you notice that?' asked the doctor.

Brain and Intelligence

Would having a bigger brain mean greater intelligence? Is not an elephant's brain bigger than a human's? One should not simply look at size and weight. The proportion of brain's weight to body weight must be taken into consideration too. By that measure, calculated as a proportion of body weight, a human's brain is relatively the biggest. Some species of dolphins come next.

Alright, then can we determine whether one is intelligent or not based on the folds in the brain? That is not entirely true. It also depends on where the folds are located. A person may have a large house. But what benefit is it if he uses just one room? Is it not important how the brain is used?

17

'What is so surprising about it?' asked Pandian.

'Human civilization has two cornerstones. One is language, the other would be hands,' said the doctor.

'Do explain in detail,' Pandian requested.

'Take the example of other animals – say a rat, for instance. Let us assume it gets caught in a mousetrap and somehow manages to escape. That rat would not come near a trap ever again. But other rats would keep getting caught in traps. What would happen if it were a human? He would share what he knows with other humans. No one would go near the mousetrap, right?'

'Yes,' Pandian nodded in agreement.

'That is the distinguishing feature of humans. Information that a human becomes aware of spreads among all other humans. Language helps achieve this. Humans write in books all that they have learnt. They impart that knowledge to their children too. Though each human has an average amount of intelligence, the combined intelligence of humanity is as vast as a boundless ocean. After he began to talk, man's brain began growing rapidly. It is language that has transformed monkey into modern man,' said the doctor.

'This Snowman can speak,' said Pandian.

'Yes. Just like speech, human's hands are important too. What all can a monkey do with its hands? It would search for lice, eat and fight. But a human draws a picture with their hands and also writes. They perform a thousand other intricate tasks. Humans were the first to work with their hands. As they kept performing the simple tasks, the hand's capabilities increased. A philosopher, Friedrich Engels, said that all the achievements of man have been made possible due to the labour of his hands.'

The doctor further explained, 'This ancestor of the snowman has not practised using his hands at all. He would not be able to use any tools or implements. So, he would neither have a home nor have clothes. He too lives like a forest monkey!'

In a soft voice, Kim said, 'Doctor Sahab, I have a doubt. Our bhikshu calls it desire. It is because of this that man does not have peace.'

'Is that so?' asked Pandian.

'Among all living beings, is it not man alone who experiences sorrows and worries? Envy and covetousness stem from desire. Disappointment and anger arise from it too,' Kim said.

'Yes. True. This is what the Buddhist philosophy states,' agreed the doctor.

'We have to win over that instinct. If we overcome desire, we will not face any kind of sorrow. Depending on how well we can overcome it, we can be happier. Our bhikshu often says so,' said Kim.

'I will never accept this. Is it not that instinctive desire that acts as the basis for all our knowledge? Is it not desire that has brought us so far in search of the Snowman?' the doctor said.

'Alright, let us start. Night is falling,' said Pandian.

They started walking and eventually reached the foot of the mountains. Night closed in.

'It is dangerous to stay at the foot of such a mountain. Big rocks stand atop the peak, split and broken. In the Himalayan regions, minor earthquakes happen all the time. Rocks then slide down and often fall. So, we must somehow reach the other side,' said the doctor.

'There is a path through the mountain. I remember seeing it,' said Kim.

Kim showed the way. Both of them followed. It grew darker. 'That day, I saw that this place was enveloped in a blue light,' Kim said.

They walked along, stumbling in the dark. After they had travelled some distance, they saw a blue light. Pandian noticed that the doctor and Kim appeared blue too. The snowy surface and the glaciers also emitted a blue light. They walked through this blue light.

Gradually, they understood where the light was

coming from. There was a blue light shining atop a rock. But it was not a lamp. It was a big, blue-coloured rock which was emitting the glow.

'Diamond … a diamond rock,' the doctor said.

Yes! It was a blue-coloured diamond. That rock was bigger than a man!

All Gods Reside in Our Hands

Since ancient times, hands have been venerated in India. They believed that all the Gods resided in the hands. Every day, after waking up, we had to look at our open palms. There is a prescribed shloka to be recited then:

Karagre vasathe Lakshmi
Kara madhye Saraswathi
Karamulathu Govinda
Prabahthe kara darshanam

The meaning of this Sanskrit shloka is as follows:

Lakshmi (Goddess of Wealth) resides in the tips of our hands.
Saraswathi (Goddess of Knowledge) in the centre of our palms.
At the base of our hands resides Govinda (Vishnu, the Preserver).
Hence, look at and pray to your hands each morning!

There is another version of this shloka where instead of '*karamulathu Govinda*', the words '*karamule Sthitha Gowri*' are chanted.

18

Pandian's eyes scrunched up. It seemed as if he was wearing blue-tinted glasses.

'Diamond! Diamond!' The doctor danced in joy.

'Such a huge diamond?' asked Pandian.

The doctor caressed that blue stone. He then put his eyes against it and looked into it. 'This is a very high-grade stone – it is a diamond of the first water. There is flawless clarity in the light inside it.'

'What does it mean?'

'Diamond is a crystal. Like salt. If a ray of light enters it, it will get refracted inside itself.'

'How?'

'Imagine a room where all four walls are mirrors. Even the floor is a mirror. The ceiling is a mirror too. What will happen if an electric light is flashed inside that room?' the doctor asked.

'Light would get reflected endlessly from one mirror to another. The reflections would dart inside here and there.'

'What would be seen if a lamp is lit there? Would it not appear as if tens of millions of lamps are lit?' the doctor asked.

'Yes!'

'Diamonds are similar. Inside a diamond, there are millions of intricate mirrored rooms. The light that falls on a diamond gets reflected inside again and again. This is referred to as the "clarity" of the diamond.'

'If that is the case, is this diamond very valuable?'

'You have heard of the "Kohinoor" diamond, right? That diamond was a part of Shah Jahan's Peacock Throne. Today, it is in the London Museum. We cannot determine its value today ... for it is invaluable. The prices may go up in so many millions. Even if one were to give billions, one cannot buy it. That diamond, however, is smaller than a hen's egg, whereas this is a thousand times bigger than that.'

'Oh, my!' Pandian stood flabbergasted.

'We can't even budge this diamond rock,' said the doctor.

Pandian got all flustered. 'Doctor, come, let us move. Let us go back immediately. We will return with the right tools and implements. Somehow or the other, we will take it.'

'What shall we do after taking it back?'

'Sell it.'

'Who can buy this? This can be bought only by wiping out the entire treasury of the American government!'

Pandian was perplexed. 'What do we do, Doctor? Such colossal treasure! What do we do with it?'

'Let us cut out a small piece from this. Even if we manage to cut out a piece the size of a hen's egg and sell it, we would be the richest men on this Earth,' said the doctor.

'Yes. That would be the right thing to do,' agreed Pandian. He ran and got his snow axe. He leapt up and hit the diamond with great force. The axe hit the diamond with a loud clang, but it was Pandian's arms that felt the pain of the hit.

'What is this?!' exclaimed the doctor.

Pandian struck harder again.

'Pandian! Stop that!' shouted the doctor. 'Look at the snow axe.'

Pandian lifted the snow axe and looked at it. It was broken beyond repair. He looked at the diamond. There was not even a small scratch on it. Pandian was dumbstruck.

The doctor laughed. 'Diamonds are very hard, Pandian. It can be broken only with a very strong tool. It cannot even be nicked with stones or iron.'

'Yes, I remember now. In Tamil there is a proverb – "only a diamond can cut a diamond".'

'Did you know that before modern tools were invented, it was only with a cheaper black diamond that other diamonds were cut. They would put a small piece of diamond at the top of an iron tool. If that were used, glass can be cut through like cutting paper. Yes. A diamond is very strong. That is why people compare durable things and resolute people to diamonds.'

'What do we do now?' asked Pandian tiredly.

'I have some nitro-glycerine. It is a very powerful explosive. Let us try using it,' said the doctor.

'Okay!'

The doctor opened his box. He took out a small, heavy bottle. There was a slightly viscous liquid inside it. 'Using this, we can make the type of explosive that we need. If a small electric current is passed through this, that is enough to result in a tremendous explosion.'

'What do we do with this?'

'Under the rock, beneath the diamond, there would be small crevices. A glass tube filled with nitro-glycerine should be put inside it. From it, an electric rod should be connected and brought out. It is enough if the battery is attached to the rod. Nitro-glycerine will explode, and the diamond will break.'

'Will it shatter and become powder?' asked Pandian doubtfully.

'This device would not have that much power. Only a few pieces would break and fall. That much is enough for us.'

It was then that Pandian noticed Kim sitting calmly. He had not even come near the diamond.

'Kim, do you not want the diamond?'

'I don't want it,' said Kim.

'Why?' asked the doctor.

'Lord Buddha is testing us. If I touch that, I will lose the Buddha's blessings,' said Kim.

The doctor put back the tube of explosive as if he had just realized something.

'What do you mean?' asked Pandian.

'We are here only to find the Snowman. Nothing enroute should divert us. If we covet the things we see on our journey, we will not be able to reach our goal, right?' said Kim.

Pandian realized the truth in Kim's words. But his desire for the diamond did not diminish.

'Lord Buddha always watches over us. He is testing our determination. Our bhikshus have given sermons on this,' said Kim.

The doctor then said, 'Yes, Pandian. This diamond is not our goal. We need to travel ahead to find the Snowman.'

'Leaving the diamond behind?' Pandian asked incredulously.

The doctor said, 'Yes, there is no other way. Come, let us proceed!'

They journeyed on.

The Diamond Market

Which is the biggest diamond in the world? It is a diamond called 'Cullinan' found in South Africa. It is slightly bigger than a hen's egg. Then, this diamond was broken into three pieces. Today, the highest number of diamonds in the world are found in Russia. In India, in the olden days, diamonds used to be found in Raichur in Karnataka and Golconda in then Andhra Pradesh. The Kohinoor diamond was found about 800 years ago in Golconda. The Hampi (Vijayanagar) market was so rich that precious stones like diamonds, rubies and emeralds were sold here.

19

Seeing Pandian walk along absentmindedly, immersed in thought, the doctor asked, 'You did not have the heart to leave the diamond and come, did you?'

'Not so. Once I stepped away from the diamond, my desire vanished. I could not think clearly in the blue light that emanated from that stone. I was giddy. I did not have any thought other than that I should take the diamond. If I think back now, I feel really foolish!'

Then he paused and asked the doctor, 'How did that diamond come there? Aren't diamonds found under the earth?'

'Diamonds are formed below the ground. The trees that have been trapped under the earth for millions of years become diamonds. Due to the tremendous heat from Earth's core, they become charcoal. And then, due to the pressure of the earth, they gradually become diamonds. Diamond, in fact, is actually just hardened coal! You knew that, right?' said the doctor.

'How would a tree go under the surface of Earth?' Pandian asked again.

'When earthquakes occur, the ground splits open. The trees that are at its edges of the rift then fall in. And earthquakes occur frequently in the Himalayan region. The reason for this diamond coming out could be an earthquake too! The earth would have split open and lava from inside might have poured out. The diamond probably surfaced then,' the doctor explained.

They walked on, crossed the mountain and reached the other side.

'It is getting late. Let us eat and stay the night here itself,' said the doctor.

Pandian noticed a cave. 'Doctor, look there! A comfortable cave! Let us stay inside it. There is no need for a tent.'

The doctor laughed. 'If you stay the night in a cave, by tomorrow morning you would be frozen and stiff like a log of wood.'

'Why?' asked Pandian, not really comprehending.

'There will be snowfall tonight. The cold wind that blows through the snow will blow inside the cave too.'

'Where else can we stay? In this barren snowfield?'

'Yes. Immediately after we build the tent, snow would fall on it. The snow on the tent would be like a big sheet,' said the doctor.

'If that is so, could we also sleep inside an ice block?'

'Yes. A block of ice would not let the cold pass through. The cold outside would be around minus twenty-five degrees Celsius. The snow slab would prevent this chill from seeping inside. The temperature inside would be above zero,' said the doctor.

Pandian pitched the tent. The doctor heated up the water. Kim tidied up and stowed the vehicle. After having their meal, they went inside the tent and slept.

A diamond appeared in Pandian's dream. It was a blue diamond. He went to pick it up. It was then that he realized that it was only blue-hued water. Suddenly, he fell headfirst into the water and sank. It was now a blue-coloured sea. On all the four sides, he could see waves of blue water. Inside it, he found fishes swimming. He gasped for breath. He could not swim at all. The blue-coloured water entered via his nose and filled his chest. It entered via his mouth and filled his stomach. He felt as if he had swallowed a big diamond. He sank deeper and deeper.

Abruptly, Pandian woke up. *What a frightful nightmare!* he thought. Pondering over the meaning of this weird dream, he went back to sleep.

It was Kim who woke up first in the morning.

After meditation, he came out and looked at the sky. Then, he looked at the peaks. Entering the tent, he cried, 'Doctor! Doctor!' and shook him awake.

The doctor woke up in alarm and asked, 'What?'

'Our tent is in a different place now! We are very far from the place where we pitched our tent yesterday!' exclaimed Kim.

Snow Houses

Inuits live close to the North Pole. They would construct houses using blocks of ice. They stacked the ice blocks and built a house in the shape of a hemisphere. It would appear like an inverted coconut shell. They would light a fire inside the house for some time. Then, the ice blocks would begin to melt. Immediately, they would put out the fire. The ice would freeze again. As a result of this process, the gaps between the ice blocks would all get filled. It would become a house made of a single unbroken block of ice. Ice is very strong. So, a house made of ice would not break easily. Ice does not let the cold from outside pass through. So, the cold inside the home would be far less than outside. The Inuits stayed in such a house.

20

Both the men woke up in terror and alarm. When they came out and looked around them, they too realized that it was a different place. The fallen snow had spread out on the floor. It was like detergent froth that would be seen while washing clothes. But it was crystallized like sugar. While walking, it came up to their knees. There was a loud crunching, like they were walking on a spread of hundreds of papads.

'The glacier on which we were has moved!' exclaimed Pandian.

'No! Look here! Someone has hammered in the pegs,' said the doctor.

'Yes,' said Pandian.

'They did not know how to tie a knot with the rope. They have simply rolled up the rope in circles. They have carried us along with the tent,' said the doctor, observing the surrounding mountains keenly. The next moment he shouted out, 'Ahh!'

'What?' asked Pandian.

'Look, we were there,' he pointed.

'Yes,' said Pandian.

'Snow has fallen quite heavily there and piled up high. Had we been there over the night, we would have been buried deep under the snow,' the doctor said.

'Somebody has saved us!' Pandian exclaimed in amazement.

'It is not easy for humans to access this area. Also, they would surely not be able to hike in the dark.'

'Then, was it the Snowman who saved us?' asked Pandian.

'It is most possibly the Snowman,' said the doctor.

'Why would he save us?' asked Pandian.

'He has never harmed anyone till now,' said the doctor.

'We need to find him. I am very eager to meet him,' said Pandian.

After a meal, they continued on their journey.

When they had crossed that mountain, Pandian suddenly cried out, 'A river!'

He was very astonished to see a big waterfall there too. They neared that river soon. As they went nearer and nearer, they realized an amazing thing – there was no sound from that waterfall!

A noiseless waterfall! How is that possible? Pandian could not believe it at all.

When they neared it, he understood. That waterfall was completely frozen. It was ice frozen and shaped like a waterfall! But it looked like flowing water. The curved shape of the waves could be seen, too, where the water must have fallen. At the same time, it was broad at the base, like the wide trunk of a tree, and gradually tapered off as it went upwards.

'How did this form?' asked Pandian.

'The water is flowing from somewhere else; it becomes cooler gradually. When it nears the fall, it becomes like ice cream. When it falls down, it freezes in the cold,' the doctor explained.

'I have not seen flowing water anywhere in this area. From where and how does the melted water come to this river?' Pandian asked.

'Let us go up and see,' said the doctor. 'We would anyway have to go there.'

'How do we go there?'

'The waterfall is not that steep. We can climb up,' said the doctor.

They took a trekking pole in one hand and an ice-axe in the other. The doctor taught Kim how to climb. First Kim and then Pandian began to climb. Using his ice-axe, Kim cut out a step-hole in the snow. He put his leg on it and climbed up. He stood there, placing the trekking pole firmly. With one hand, he cut out the next step. Then, he climbed onto that step.

Thus, they went up slowly. On reaching the top, Pandian unwound the rope that he had tied to his waist. The doctor tied up their things at the other end of the rope. Pandian and Kim pulled the rope up and took the things. Then they held onto the rope tightly as the doctor climbed up. Once he had reached the others, he observed the area keenly. There was a river above the waterfall. It was frozen too.

As they went ahead, the river began to change. At first it was ice, then in the middle there was some ice-cream-like snow. As they went further, they found the ice to be more thawed.

They went ahead on their way. The banks of the river were frozen. They could see blue water flowing in the middle.

'Water!' exclaimed Pandian.

'There is a hot spring here somewhere,' said the doctor. 'Hot springs are found in places where there are volcanoes and frequent earthquakes. In other places, the lava is present very deep inside the earth. It has come to the surface here. Lava is the hot liquid found beneath the ground, it is molten rock. Its temperature would be several thousand degrees Celsius. It is enough even if a small portion of its heat comes up. The water above the surface would start boiling.'

They neared the hot spring.

Is Earth a Ball of Liquid?

What is this Earth, on which we are living, made of? We are living on the upper surface of Earth. Plants grow on its surface too. The roots of trees, at the most, can go 100 feet deep. Water can be found at up to 1,000 feet. The distance of 34–40 km below Earth's visible surface is called the crust – this is the hard material. Underneath that, is the mantle – the temperature here is high enough for the rocks to melt, but because of the intense pressure from above, it remains solid. The flow here is like very thick honey. This is present for a depth of almost 2,900 km. Below this layer is a liquid mass, called the outer core. This is approximately 2,250 km in diameter. The innermost layer of Earth is called the inner core. It is a hard substance made of iron and nickel. It is a common misconception that the major portion of Earth is a liquid mass!

21

A gust of warm breeze suddenly touched them. The ice was completely thawed and water could be seen flowing in the river.

'We have reached,' said the doctor.

In the space between the two banks, hot water was bubbling. They crossed over to the other side, climbing over the rocks. It was a very beautiful scene. On all four sides, polished stones stood in a circle. In its midst, pristine blue water lay pooled. The water was crystal clear. The bottom of the pool seemed very close.

'Time for a bath,' declared Pandian exuberantly.

'Wait. Let me first check how hot the water is,' said the doctor. He felt the water and declared, 'Perfect temperature!'

Bubbles popped on the surface of the water. Steam kept rising. It dawned on Pandian that since the beginning of this journey, this was the first time they were removing their clothes.

They bathed in the water. Once their body sank deeper into the water, it was extremely soothing. The human skin wrinkles in the bitter cold, and the sweat pores close up. As the skin is not exposed to the elements, it grows pale. But when hot water touched them, they felt rejuvenated.

'Let us not go ashore at all! Let us just keep swimming here,' said Pandian.

'You would want to come ashore soon. There is a reason,' the doctor laughed.

After some time, Pandian understood what the doctor meant. He began to feel slightly hungry at first. Then, he grew really ravenous. Eventually, he could not control his hunger pangs!

'I am starving,' declared Pandian.

'Your body has become warm. Your muscle fibres have relaxed. Blood flow has increased. This is equivalent to running for several kilometres.'

They climbed ashore. Pandian ate till he was about to burst. Immediately, his eyes drooped. Sleep overcame him and he grew light-headed. Without even pitching the tent, they simply spread it out and fell asleep on it.

Someone woke them up. Pandian opened his eyes. He sprang up, alert.

Two Buddhist monks were standing near them. Their heads were completely shaved. They were wearing saffron robes. Kim fell at their feet, bowed and greeted them.

'May Lord Buddha shower his blessings on you,' the monks blessed him.

Pandian and the doctor clasped their palms together in greeting.

'Who are you? Why have you come here?' asked one of the monks.

'We have come here in search of the Snowman,' replied Pandian.

'We are coming from Tibet. We are an order of Buddhist monks from Tibet. Our huge Buddhist monastery is there. It is called Siva-o-Repa. Our guru is the head lama there. His name is Mila Shepatorje, which means "smiling diamond". He is now one hundred and forty years old.'

'One hundred and forty years?' Truly?' Pandian asked, astonished.

'It is very common for people in Tibet to live up to a hundred years. Some of our lamas have lived even up to one hundred and twenty years,' said the monk.

'Would your Maha Lama, the leader of the order, even be able to stand up? Would he be an incapacitated old man?'

The monk asked laughingly, 'Looking at me, how old would you judge me to be?'

'Forty or forty-five,' replied Pandian.

'I am going to be ninety soon!' said the bhikshu, smiling.

Pandian drew in a sharp breath. The monk had a mouth full of strong teeth. His shoulders were broad and strong. His hands were firm and sinewy. His stomach was tight and curved in. His face was unlined.

'Unbelievable!' said Pandian.

'Tibet's Buddhist religion sect is called Vajrayana, which prescribes a number of meditative practices.'

'What is your reason for coming here?' the doctor inquired.

'Last year, our Maha Lama summoned us. He said that he would part with his life in ten years.'

'How does he know that?' asked Pandian.

'He will die only when he desires. Death will not come to him when he does not want it to,' said the other monk.

The first monk said, 'Our Maha Lama ordered us to come here. That is why we came.'

'Why?' asked Pandian.

'Searching for our next lama,' said the bhikshu.

Who Are the Lamas?

The Tibetan Plateau is high up on the Himalayan mountains. Some countries in the Tibetan Plateau were under the British rule. Today, Tibet is governed as an autonomous region of China.

There are no kings in Tibet. There, the religious leader is the king. He is called lama. He is the leader of all the Buddhist monks. Lama means 'principal guru'.

Tibetan people rebelled against the Chinese occupation of their land. Their leader, Dalai Lama, escaped from Tibet and sought refuge in India. He has travelled around the world seeking to spread the message of universal peace and the Buddhist religion. He has also been awarded the Nobel Peace Prize.

22

Pandian asked in confusion, 'Here? In this snowy mountain?'

'We do not know. It is our guru's command. His spiritual signs were all correct. We reached here at last, after following them. It has been four months now since we came here,' said one monk.

On seeing that Pandian was still bewildered, the doctor explained. 'This is a practice of Tibet's Buddhist religion. Astrologers and the monks would together meditate and choose their next lama. During meditation, they would come to know of the birthplace of the next lama. They would go there, bring him and crown him as their next Maha Lama. Generally, they find young boys. But, sometimes, they even bring a child who is not even a year old, and crown him their lama.'

'Where would your next lama be?' asked Pandian.

'Our Maha Lama directed us to come here. There is a mountain to the north of this place. There would be three boulders next to each other at the foot of that mountain.

He instructed us to stand there. He foretold that our next Maha Lama would appear there,' the monk said.

'How would he look like?' asked Pandian.

'We do not know that. He would be holding a lotus flower in his hands. That lotus would be the colour of gold,' said the monk.

'Golden colour? Do you refer to the red colour as golden?' asked the doctor.

'No. Our Maha Lama showed us the golden bowl from which he would eat his food. He described that the lotus would be of that colour. That is the sign. The name of the new lama is Mila Padma Rebo. He would also be known as Bodhisattva Padmapani. It means "the Bodhisattva holding a lotus flower".'

'A golden-coloured lotus flower? I have not heard of such a thing till now.'

'We are not concerned about that. It is our guru's instruction. One among us is right now on guard near that rock. We are resting here. At night, he will come here, and one of us will go there in his stead. We will guard that place day and night,' said the monk.

'How long would you stand guard like that?' asked Pandian.

'Till Bodhisattva Padmapani appears here, or till we all die,' replied the monk.

'But our guru's prophecy will come true. Mila Padma Rebo will surely appear. Our Maha Lama is a man of great wisdom who knows the past, present and future.'

Pandian was astonished. A golden-coloured lotus? There is nothing like that. These monks would freeze to death here. But Pandian realized that he could not convince them otherwise. They were strong in their faith. No matter what he argued, they would not listen. So, he did not say anything.

'Alright. Let us talk about your quest. Tell us what you know about this Snowman that you are going in search of,' said the monk.

'He is a monkey man. He is of a species that has evolved between monkeys and humans,' said the doctor.

The monk smiled. 'There are numerous references about him in our secret manuscripts. He is called Yeti,' he said.

'Yeti?'

'Yes. Yeti means the same thing both in Sanskrit and our language – the one who has conquered all desires. He who is pure of heart, without anger or hatred. He who has infinite love towards all living beings. Only revered saints are called yetis. But our ancestors have called even these snowmen yetis,' the monk said.

'Has anything been told about where they live?' The doctor asked.

'They live in the topmost point of the Himalayan peaks. It is the purest place in this whole world. Dirt does not exist there. Nor does evil. There is nothing there that lacks beauty. Once, eons ago, our Earth was entirely like that. But due to Maran's conspiracies, the world was filled with dirty and evil things,' the monk said.

'Maran? Who is that?' Pandian asked.

'Didn't Kim say that day? The desire to come up in life pushing aside all morals. The Buddhist people believe that there is an evil power that spreads such a selfish desire in the human hearts, who is called Maran. They believe that the emotions like anger, greed, envy, sadness that humans feel were all created by this Maran.'

'So, they are saying that the idea that we should always keep succeeding and evolving is spreading in us due to this Maran, right? So, isn't this power called Maran the reason behind the evolution of apes into men of today?' Pandian asked.

'Yes, that power secretly lies in all our hearts. That is why we are never satisfied no matter what we have. Call anybody in this world and ask them what they need. Everyone will have a huge list of wants. It was due to this desire that man tamed and domesticated beasts, tortured them like slaves to do his work and accumulated wealth,' the monk said.

'That's true,' the doctor agreed.

'You are saying that man is an evolved form of an ape. But is this evolution? Aren't they killing millions of people by nuclear bombs? Is this civilization? Will any other monkey kill thousand other monkeys? Even crows share the food they get. But people watch their fellow people die of hunger while they themselves are in lavish palaces living an exorbitant life. Yes, friends! Evolution has only spread evil. And Maran is the reason,' the monk said.

'Okay, let us assume that the world is now full of evil due to this Maran's power. So, is there no evil in the place where the yetis live?' the doctor asked.

'Tibetan religious texts call the place where they live as the Dharmasthala. Maran can never gain entry there. So, there is no evil there. Nor is there any sadness. It is a place full of beauty, happiness and goodness,' the monk said.

'Why did the Buddha save only one place like that?' Pandian asked.

The monk smiled at him.

What Is a Yeti?

The creature that people call the Yeti is a legend that comes from Tibetan and Sherpa folklore. It is also called the Abominable Snowman. The word 'yeti' comes from the Tibeto-Burman words *yeh* and *teh* – 'yeh' means rocky place and 'teh' means bear. So, it literally translates to rocky bear.

In the recent years, scientists have tested the footprints and hair that supposedly belong to yeti. Most of these belong to the rare subspecies of the Himalayan brown bear or Asian black bear. Despite all of these modern science claims, yeti remains a popular legend in the folklores and people do believe in it.

23

'Before I answer this question, I need to tell you about a rite we undertake in Tibet,' said the monk, and began to explain.

'Floods and earthquakes would often occur in Tibet. Crops would be completely wiped out. So, after each harvest, we would set aside a small portion of the grains we harvested. We would dry that portion out completely, and put it in a copper container. Then we would close it and seal it by pouring molten lead, and place that container high up on a mountain peak.'

'Why?' asked Pandian, interrupting.

'What would we do if, at any point of time, an earthquake or flood occurred and our agricultural output was entirely destroyed? We would need seeds to restart farming, would we not? This rite was to ensure that. Many a time, our crops have been destroyed like this. We would then scale up the mountain, retrieve the container and take out the seed grains. We would then plant them afresh. These yetis are also like those seeds,' said the monk.

'I am still not able to figure it out,' said Pandian.

'Evil has increased in this world. What would happen if the entire world is destroyed one day? What to do if not even a single human is left alive? It is exactly for this reason that the Buddha has given special protection to the yetis. When the world is destroyed, the Buddha will bring them back down. They will populate Earth again. A new humankind would originate from them. Those humans would not know evil,' said the monk.

'Is there anything mentioned in your manuscripts about the way of getting there?' asked the doctor.

'Nobody should go there. Those who go there cannot return. To reach there, first you need to walk over the sea, then you need to walk on fire. This is what our holy books mention.'

Tall stories! Pandian thought. *How can one walk over the sea? Over fire? How can there even be a sea atop the Himalayas?*

'We have travelled this far in search of the Snowman. We need to go there,' said the doctor.

'That is your wish. No one can hinder another's journey. You have our blessings,' the monks said in unison.

Taking leave of the monks, the three of them started the journey again.

They kept walking on the snowy plains.

After travelling for a really long distance over the snow, they reached the base of a peak. Using a rope, they climbed up. When they reached the top and looked across, the three of them gasped in astonishment. There was a huge sea on the other side!

'Sea?' exclaimed Pandian.

'Yes. It is a sea. But the sea has frozen over. This is for sure a really huge sheet of ice,' the doctor said.

'I remember this icy expanse. Carrying me in his arms, the Snowman quickly slid across here,' Kim said, his excitement showing through.

'In which direction had he gone?' the doctor asked.

'There! You can see a mountain split into two. There is a gap near it. He went through that,' Kim said.

They reached the sea.

'How did a sea appear atop the Himalayas?' Pandian asked in transparent astonishment.

The doctor said, 'Sixty-five million years ago, the Himalayan region was under the sea. The area beyond the Himalayas was the Laurasian continent. The land mass that is now India was then a part of the continent called Gondwanaland. When the hot, molten lava at the core of Earth began to cool down, the planet shrank – the way an orange's skin shrinks when it dries up. It was then that all the continents on Earth began to separate. India got detached and dashed against Laurasia. Immediately, the earth folded over and rose up, becoming the Himalayas.

The sea water that was already there flowed out. But all four sides of this area are surrounded by mountains. So, the sea water was not able to flow out, and has remained like water standing stagnant in a huge pit.'

'So, this is a part of the ocean. We can consider this as a small fragment of the sea?' asked Pandian.

'Yes. When the landmass rose up as a mountain, the temperatures dropped and became cold. Hence, this sea became frozen,' the doctor explained.

They had reached the frozen sea.

'Rig Veda is the oldest book in India. In it, India is referred to as "Jambudweepam", which means the "island of jambu trees". But India is a peninsula. Why was it then referred to as an island?' asked the doctor.

Pandian asked, 'Why?'

'In ancient times, there was a sea even to the north of India. Our ancestors were aware of that,' said the doctor.

'How do we even cross this sea? It seems to extend really far!' asked Pandian.

'We would need to slide across. You know how to slide on snow right?' asked the doctor.

'I have received training for that,' said Pandian. 'Do you know how to?' he asked, looking at Kim.

'Just say the word, I will slide,' said Kim confidently.

'Alright, let us start,' said the doctor.

A Plant That Glows

Kalidas wrote a famous epic poem called *Raghuvamsam*. The main protagonist's name is Raghu.

In the fourth chapter of *Raghuvamsam*, there are descriptions of Raghu winning all the kingdoms of India. He conquered many places, from the Pandya kingdom in the south to the Himalayas in the north. He annexed all kingdoms from Kamarupa (modern Assam) to Persia.

In this particular chapter, Kalidas describes in detail all the regions of India. This is very helpful to learn about ancient India.

There is some interesting information in the seventieth verse. Raghu went with an army and won against the mountain tribes in the Himalayan regions. There was a plant in that region. Apparently, it glowed like a lamp at night. In that light, the chains of Raghu's elephants shone bright. What plant is that? Till today, nobody has found such a plant.

But all the other facts that Kalidas mentions about the other areas are accurate. If that is so, then such a plant could have existed too. There could have been many such rare varieties of plants in the Himalayas.

24

The surface of the sea was even. Hence, they were able to slide over it really fast. Pandian recollected that the monk's statement – that one needed to walk on the sea – had turned out to be true.

Beneath the ice, it was like a real sea. Shoals of silver-coloured fish could be seen frozen in the ice. Striped water snakes were also seen. A very big boa snake seemed to be frozen mid-swim. It was the biggest kind of snake in the world. It was five times as long as Pandian, and with a girth as wide as him. Had this been a regular sea, the three of them would have become its prey by now.

'Aren't boa snakes currently found near the equator?' asked Pandian.

'Yes. But, perhaps, a long time ago, this sea was part of that sea in the area near the equator.'

'How long ago was it alive?'

'It has been millions of years since the Himalayas rose. Even after that, it could have lived in this sea. Gradually, as the height of the Himalayas increased and the cold became intense, this boa snake would have died. Even by a conservative estimate, this creature is millions of years old,' the doctor said.

Pandian thought that some event would have occurred, freezing the sea in a year or so. Inside the water, the sea plants lay still like a dense forest. They were frozen too. In places where there were no sea plants, many types of fishes could be seen clearly. Some were round, like pillows. Some were like long swords. Some were shaped like boats. Multi-hued fishes were there – pale blue, red, yellow. That icy surface was like a beautiful painting. Suddenly, in a particular place, bodies of whales could be seen. Several whales had frozen in ice with their mouths wide open.

Pandian exclaimed in surprise, 'These whales have legs!'

It was true! Those whales had legs like a lizard's. The back legs were larger, while the front legs were smaller.

'Whales are actually mammals. They suckle their young. Tens of millions of years ago, they lived on the land. They belonged to the reptile family just like dinosaurs. Then, they began to drift into the sea and live there. But they still cannot breathe underwater. Other fishes swallow water in and breathe out through their gills. By doing this, they get the necessary oxygen. But whales open their mouths outside the water and take in the oxygen they need. In the beginning, they had big legs. Once they began to live in the sea, gradually, they had no use for the legs. Hence, in the course of evolution, their legs disappeared,' said the doctor.

'Have the legs of these creatures not disappeared yet?' Pandian asked.

'Yes. They lived millions of years ago. This is a small sea, isn't it? Therefore, they might have gone to the shore often and hunted and eaten small animals,' said the doctor.

Pandian was very astonished. How would it be if a whale went ashore and hunted? They would almost be like crocodiles.

They went very fast, sliding down the ice. Pandian realized that they had travelled very far. At last, they reached the base of the split peak. They could see the shore there.

'It was that shore!' exclaimed Kim.

They neared the shore, where lay many kinds of boulders and rocks. When they reached the shore, they removed the ski-boards from their legs. They pulled the vehicle there and stopped it.

Kim said, 'We have to travel a great distance through those rocks.'

'Let us eat something first,' said the doctor.

They heated up the water and began to eat their food.

Then, they saw some men walking on the sea. They were rather tall. But their hands and legs were very short.

They walked slowly, swaying from side to side. They were not clearly visible.

'Doctor, look there!' cried Pandian.

'They are not snowmen. Snowmen are even taller,' said the doctor.

'If so, who are they?' Pandian asked.

'Come, let us see,' said the doctor.

They got up and went near those men. As the light falling on the ice was glaring against their eyes, they could not see the men clearly; they seemed like shadows. Those men were breaking the ice and boring holes in it.

'Why are they drilling holes in the ice?' asked Pandian.

'The ice near the shores would be thinner. It is easier to drill there. It would not be that cold under the ice. Some small fishes might still live there. I guess they are trying to catch them,' the doctor replied.

Pandian immediately understood the logic. In the ice that they had walked over, there were several small cracks. Under such cracks, small fishes stood unmoving, with their mouths tightly closed. In the depths, water could be seen in its liquid form.

'A little amount of air enters the water through the minor cracks in the ice. Due to that, very small amounts of oxygen mix with the water. These small fishes live by breathing that oxygen,' said the doctor.

They reached the people who were catching the fishes. Pandian yelled in shock. 'They are not humans. They are crocodiles!'

They were, in fact, crocodiles. But they stood straight, bearing down heavily on their back legs and tails. Two of the crocodiles were digging in the ice using their forelegs. One crocodile looked at them and gave a terrible growl. Immediately, the other crocodiles noticed them too and leapt towards them.

Pandian saw them running on two legs like humans. The three of them began to run helter-skelter. But the crocodiles ran faster than them. It seemed as if they would catch them in a few seconds.

'Run zig-zag. Crocodiles can run only in a straight line,' the doctor shouted, running.

They ran zig-zag. The crocodiles that came chasing them stumbled. Some even fell down on the ice. They escaped and reached the shore. But many more crocodiles appeared from behind the boulders on the shore. Climbing atop the rocks, they shook their hands and snarled.

'That's it. We are finished!' said the doctor.

They stood still.

'If we had gunpowder, we could have tried to burst the explosive. But it is in the vehicle,' said the doctor frantically.

Swinging their hands, the crocodiles surrounded the trio in a circle. Inside their mouths, dense rows of huge teeth gleamed menacingly.

Just then, a terrible noise filled the air. It was like ten elephants trumpeting together.

Legs Can Become Hands Too!

Human's legs are used exclusively for walking. So, the mid portion of the feet became arched. The big toe got separated and became strong. It enables us to keep our feet firmly on the ground and walk well.

But some tribal communities still use their legs the way monkeys do. Mikhlo Ha Mikhlai, an anthropologist, researched on the Papuan tribal people. They live in Melanesia (north of Australia).

'Papuan people pick things up using their legs. They perform various other tasks using their legs. They catch fish from the water using their legs. They even peel a banana with their legs and eat it!' Mikhlai mentions.

With practice, the limbs of our body can be trained the way we want.

25

On hearing that noise, all the crocodiles were frightened. They scattered and began running in all four directions. They dashed against each other, tripped over one another and fell, howling in fear.

Again, the trumpeting noise sounded. The three shook with fear on hearing it. All the crocodiles ran away and disappeared rapidly. The three men looked in the direction from which the sound arose. At first, a shadow fell on the rocks. It was gigantic. It seemed like a huge rakshasa's shadow. Then, from behind a huge boulder, a huge, towering monkey rose. It was almost 12 feet in height. It looked taller than two men standing atop one another!

Its body was fully covered with soft, thick, ash grey fur. Its body was like that of humans. But its hands looked different. The back of its hands also had thick fur. Its fingers were short and thick. Its legs were squat and bent.

'Yeti,' said Kim. He suddenly took a step forward.

He immediately went down on his knees and bowed his head respectfully.

'Snowman!' said the doctor.

No words came out of Pandian, who was dumbfounded.

The Snowman's face was not like that of a monkey. It was like a human's face, but hairier. His eyes were beautiful, like glass spheres. They shone with a bright light, like two pale blue diamonds. He did not have any lips. His jaw was not protruding like that of a monkey. But it was not like a human face either, with a moustache and beard. Instead, soft, ash-grey hair grew thick on his face. In its midst, was a small mouth. Inside the mouth were small white teeth in an even row. He did not have canine teeth like those of monkeys and other animals. Hence, his face was similar to a human's.

The Snowman looked at each of them in turn. Then, he jumped from the boulder and picked something from a rock crevice. It was a big fruit. He put it on a rock and looked at them. Then he pointed at the fruit and then at his mouth. The doctor understood that he was asking them to eat.

The Snowman then said something. Hearing his voice, the three of them were awash with pleasure. The voice was neither like a human's nor like an animal's. It was like a very big harmonium being played fast. They were not able to guess whether it was a song or regular speech or music. But it was very, very sweet. Then, the

Snowman jumped and reached another rock. Then he went far away, nimbly jumping over the rocks. Gradually, he disappeared.

'The Snowman is showing us his hospitality,' said the doctor.

They went near the fruit. It was the size of a large pumpkin.

The doctor cut it with his knife. Immediately, a very sweet aroma rose out of it – like the fragrance of mango mingled with that of a lotus bloom.

'What fruit is this?' asked Pandian.

'I do not know. I have neither seen such a fruit anywhere nor heard about it.'

At first, it appeared to be a fruit of the melon variety. But the inside had fleshy arils like a jackfruit's. Kim picked up an aril.

'Don't eat that. It is a fruit unknown to us till now. Let us test it first before eating,' said the doctor.

'Even if the Snowman gives me poison, I will eat it happily,' said Kim, putting it into his mouth. His face brightened.

Pandian and the doctor pulled apart the arils and ate them. They had never eaten such a sweet fruit until then. It was very sugary but with a hint of tartness. It was as if the sweet jackfruit had been mixed with honey. If someone had claimed that such a fruit existed in the world, they would not have believed them before that moment. It was that delicious! They ate the arils by turns. Even after eating a lot, they did not feel sickly sweet.

Once they had finished eating, Pandian said, 'My taste buds are not satisfied. I feel like eating up this peel too.'

'I wonder if this is a fruit or *amrit* – the food of gods,' the doctor said.

'Let us follow the Snowman,' said Pandian.

They darted between the rocks. They were able to move fast. Pandian went first, jumping from one rock to another.

Suddenly, Pandian realized one thing. No matter how high he jumped, his breath did not catch. He did not feel even a bit tired. 'Doctor, this fruit is really divine nectar. After eating this, I feel no tiredness.'

The doctor appeared lost in deep thought.

'What are you thinking, Doctor?' asked Pandian.

'Where did this fruit grow? It was really very sweet. Only fruits ripened by the sun would be this sweet. Where did this fruit come from?' the doctor wondered aloud.

'Yes. This is a mystery,' said Pandian.

'Somewhere around here, there is a place with green foliage. The Snowman lives there,' said the doctor.

'How can plants grow on snowy peaks?' questioned Pandian.

'That is what we need to find. Let us explore,' said the doctor.

'Alright, Doctor. How did the crocodile men evolve?' Pandian asked.

'They are not crocodile men. They are crocodiles. We assumed that they were men because they walked erect,' said the doctor.

'How did they manage to walk erect?' Pandian asked.

'All crocodiles can stand up and walk erect. When necessary, even the common crocodiles in our towns and villages can get up and run fast on two legs. But they mostly stay in water, near which they get their food too. So, there is normally no need for them to get up and run. But here, the sea has frozen. They need to walk on the ice to catch fishes. Hence, gradually, they have begun to walk.'

They crossed the cluster of rocks and faced a mountain slope again. They began to climb.

'Aha!' exclaimed the doctor.

'What, Doctor?' asked Pandian.

'Now I realize which species the Snowman is!' the doctor said.

'Which species is he?' asked Pandian.

'His face is not like that of a monkey. But his body is like that of an ape. This kind of monkey man has a unique name in the history of evolution,' explained the doctor.

'What name?' asked Pandian.

'*Ramapithecus*,' replied the doctor.

'*Ramapithecus*?' queried Pandian.

'Yes. It means "Rama's tailless monkey",' said the doctor.

Ginormous Monkey Men

A researcher named G.H.R. von Koenigswald purchased monkey teeth at an apothecary in Hong Kong. Some of them were quite big! These were the teeth of huge monkey men who lived in the southern part of China. They named it *Gigantopithecus*. It means monster monkeys. It is believed that these creatures could have lived in the northern part of India too. They are also known as Meganthropus – enormous monkey.

Some bones of these huge monkeys have been found too.

26

'Rama's monkeys?! Are you referring to the *vanaras*?' Pandian asked.

'Yes. Millions of years ago, in the northern part of India, there flowed a river called the Shivalik. Many monkey men lived on its shores then,' said the doctor.

'I have never heard of such a river,' said Pandian.

'Do you know that the it was ten times bigger than the Ganga?' the doctor asked.

'How did that much water come to be there?' asked Pandian.

'The Indian continent had just then merged with Laurasia. All the waters there flowed into India, became the river Shivalik and flowed into the ocean.

'Alright,' said Pandian.

'Because of the tectonic force between the continents, the Himalayas gradually rose – and became like a dam. Hence, water could not come from Laurasia. Eventually, the Shivalik River dried up. The monkey men who lived there also gradually relocated to other places. Do you know where the banks of the Shivalik River are located in today's world?' the doctor asked.

'Where?' asked Pandian.

'The banks rose in altitude and became a mountain range that we know as the Shivalik range,' said the doctor.

'A river bank transformed into a mountain?!' asked Pandian in astonishment.

'Even today, the Himalayan ranges rise ten centimetres in height each year. Over the course of millions of years, they would have risen several kilometres in height. That is how the Shivalik River's banks became a mountain range,' said the doctor.

'Who discovered this?' asked Pandian.

'G.E. Lewis from America. He was a geologist. In 1932, he began to dig on the peaks of the Shivalik range. Everybody ridiculed him. They wondered why someone would dig on a mountain peak. But Lewis found an ancient skeleton of a monkey man there,' said the doctor.

'Is that so?' asked Pandian.

'G.E. Lewis proved that monkey men lived in India. He named such monkey men *Ramapethicus*.'

'If that is so, did the vanaras mentioned in the Ramayana really exist?' asked Pandian.

'The Ramayana was written several thousand years later. It is not known whether monkey men existed then. But perhaps people would have known about the monkey men in the form of tales told over generations. Based on that, Valmiki could have written his story,' said the doctor.

Kim stood up suddenly and addressed the doctor, 'I can hear a strange sound.'

The doctor heard it too. It was like the growl of some animal.

'What animal is that?' asked Pandian.

'There are no animals here. It is snow that makes such a sound,' the doctor said.

Kim said urgently, 'If snow growls, that means the mountain is going to swallow us up. My father used to say that snow growls only when it is hungry.'

'What Kim says is true. Pandian, run! Let us run towards the edge of that rock. This floor of ice is going to split and slide,' said the doctor.

The three of them began to run. The growling noise of the snow increased. It distorted into a terrible trumpeting sound.

'The entire snow mountain is going to break and fall,' said the doctor.

Pandian shouted, 'Doctor! Throw me the rope.'

The doctor immediately took the pipe that would throw the spike from his vehicle. He added the explosive to it.

'Faster!' said Pandian.

'Pandian, you shoot this. It should latch onto the rock's edge there. If the spike falls anywhere else, we cannot escape,' said the doctor.

Pandian took aim and detonated the pipe. He was an expert in firearms. His aim was perfect. The spike latched.

'Hold tight!' Pandian shouted.

By then, the snow mountain began to quake and tremble. The snowy ground on which they were standing began to shake too.

The doctor tied the vehicle to the rope. He also tied his body to the rope. With a terrible noise, the snowy mountain split and slid over the ice. A deafening sound tore their eardrums. The glacier had broken and fallen with an ear-splitting noise. It was akin to a thousand waterfalls plunging down simultaneously with great force. Even the glacier they stood on had split and was falling. The three of them were tied to the rope and were swaying on that. They closed their eyes in fear. Snow kept sliding down around them.

After a really long time, they opened their eyes. There was no snow there – only rocks the colour of sawdust. The landscape appeared completely different. All the ice had shattered and plummeted down.

'We escaped!' said Pandian.

'Let us climb,' said the doctor.

All of them climbed up via the rope and reached the top of the rock. They pulled up their vehicle too.

'It is fortunate that this rock was strong enough. If not, by this time, we too would have fallen down and got buried in the abyss.'

'The snow accumulated on the top of the mountain would always be soft and flow down. Hence the snow would not be tight and would be cascading down. That is why our spike pierced the rock inside. This is the reason we escaped.'

'Is what we witnessed just now called an avalanche?' asked Pandian.

'Yes.'

'How does this occur?' Pandian asked.

'When the cold increases, the ice floor becomes heavy. The soft snow inside is not able to bear the weight. Hence it cracks and explodes,' said the doctor.

Then, they climbed up the mountain. All the snow that had been there had fallen down. Hence, it was mostly muddy slush.

The doctor bent down and observed the muddy slush.

'What are you looking at, Doctor?' asked Pandian.

'Did you notice this mud? It is alluvial soil,' said the doctor.

'Yes.'

'It was a riverbank once upon a time,' said the doctor.

Where Did the Vanaras Live?

The Ramayana written by Valmiki is the oldest epic of India. Hence it is called *adi kaviyam* (first epic).

In the Kishkintha chapter, details about monkey men are mentioned. In the thirty-seventh canto, the areas where the vanaras lived are mentioned. It is mentioned that the monkey men lived in Mahendra Giri to the south of the Vindhya Mountains. In the north, they lived in the Himalayas, Kailash Mountains, Shwetha Mountains and Mandira Mountains. The vanaras living on the Anjana (Black) Mountains were blue in colour. The ones living in the Manaloya Caves were yellow in colour. The ones living in the Himalayas and Kailash Mountains were light red in colour. The monkey men who live in the Himalayas consume alcohol in excess.

This is how the Ramayana describes them.

27

The doctor then explained how the lakes formed on the Himalayas. 'The Shivalik River had disappeared right? When the Himalayas rose, water from the river pooled in its folds. That is how several lakes formed on the Himalayas. The largest among them is Mansarovar,' he said.

'Are these the banks of the Shivalik River?' asked Pandian in wonder. They walked through the muddy slush. In some places, the slush reached their knees. In some places, bubbles could be seen rising from the slush.

'Do not walk over the places from where the bubbles arise. The slush there can be very loose,' said the doctor.

Suddenly, the doctor's legs sank deep into the slush. With a terrible cry, he fell in. In the blink of an eye, Pandian threw the spike he was holding towards the doctor. It caught onto the doctor's shirt. By then, the doctor had sunk up to his neck in the slush. Pandian and Kim pulled at the rope.

The doctor came up, spattering. 'Thank God! If

Pandian had thrown the spike a few seconds later, I would not have been saved.'

When they pulled the doctor up, the slush stirred. The slush from the bottom came to the surface. There were several fish bones there.

'Fishes of the Shivalik,' said Pandian.

There was a skull lying nearby. The doctor explained that it belonged to the *Ramapithecus* species of monkey men. '*Ramapithecus* had lived here. But, at that time, this was not a mountain. Then, that species became extinct.'

The three of them started on their way again. The doctor melted some ice and cleaned up his clothes. Then they continued walking on the icy expanse. They reached the other side of the mountain, where the ground was covered by snowpack.

They sat down at one spot and had their meal for the night. They put up the tent there itself and settled for the night.

The next day, they woke up and began to walk again. They reached a lake in which the waters of the Shivalik River lay pooled and frozen. The surface of the lake was frozen like glass. They walked over it.

Suddenly, Kim's voice rose in a scream. The icy surface on which they were standing broke like fragile glass. Pandian leapt and caught hold of Kim. By then, the ice under his feet broke too. A rumbling noise sounded, and the ice began to crack.

The three of them fell down the cracks. It was as if they were falling into a deep pit. Thankfully, there was only soft snow in the place where they fell. As they fell on that, they did not get hurt. Debris from the frozen ice on which they had been standing fell on them. Those ice crystals were sharp. When they fell on Kim's ear, they tore at it and it bled. They all stood up. The snow was so soft that they sank up to their hips.

'How to extricate ourselves from here? Have we not fallen really deep?' asked Pandian.

'This is a cave. There are many such snow caves here on the snow mountains,' said the doctor.

'Fortunately, our vehicle also fell down along with us. Let us take out our equipment and throw the spike,' said Pandian.

'It is of no use. There is no rock at the top. It is only ice. If we throw the spike, the ice there would get dislodged and more of it will fall down on us,' said the doctor.

'What do we do now? Isn't the rim of the pit really high?' said Pandian.

'Let us see. This is not just a pit. This is a cave. There would surely be another opening into the cave,' said the doctor. He then pointed at the floor. It seemed as if a river had frozen. That river of ice seemed to be flowing towards the east.

'This means something. There is an opening there. The river flowed out through that,' said Pandian. He felt energized.

'Yes. Come on. Let us go in the direction of this river,' said the doctor. They went pushing their vehicle.

It felt as if they were walking over a river.

'Now I understand what happened,' said the doctor. 'This is a huge underground cave. Rocks form when lava from deep inside the ground spouts out and cools. There are several substances in lava. The softer substances disintegrated over a period of time. The place where they had been became a big cave. This is known as lava tube or lava cave,' explained the doctor.

'How did this river form here?' asked Pandian.

'The place where we had been standing was a big lake. This lava cave formed under the lake. Immediately, water began to run there and flow somewhere else. That is this river,' said the doctor.

Then, they heard a noise. It sounded as if someone was whistling very loudly.

'What noise is that?' asked Pandian.

'This lava cave bends and curves along. When air blows through it, such a sound is heard,' explained the doctor.

They walked inside the lava cave. The cave was very big. The frozen river on the floor was white. Other than that, it was very dark.

'I can hear someone speaking here,' said Pandian.

They observed keenly. It seemed as if someone was talking.

'No one is speaking. It is the sound made by ice crystals melting and dripping down,' said the doctor.

Then that noise changed into the sound of rain. After some time, it sounded like the rhythm of a tabla. Then, the sound of air changed into that of music from the flute.

'This is how the music festival of rakshasas sound!' said Pandian.

The cave became even darker. The blackness had increased.

'Take out the lamp,' said the doctor.

Kim took out the lamp. When he switched it on, light spread inside the cave. Then, they saw a wonderful sight.

Brahma's Heart

A lake on a Himalayan peak is called Mansarovar. This can be translated as 'lake of the mind'.

This is formed of pristine, clear water. Hence, the puranas call it 'Brahma's heart'.

There are several references to this lake in the Himalayas. It is mentioned that people like Parashuram and Vasishta meditated here. It is also mentioned that Arjuna visited this place.

It is very difficult to undertake a pilgrimage to Mansarovar. One must obtain special permission and walk a long distance to reach it. But, each year, many people go there. It is believed that bathing in this lake cleanses one of all sins.

28

The light from the doctor's electric lamp lit up the cave. The ice reflected it like a mirror. The light suffused and filled every available space. Pandian, who looked up at the ceiling of the cave, was stupefied.

From the ceiling hung white-coloured icicles like the roots of a banyan tree. It looked like an ornamental chandelier. Some icicles looked as if swords had been hung there. Some icicles were like big pillars. When the light fell on them, they shimmered bright. Among the icicles, pale blue-coloured ones could be seen. Red and yellow icicles could be seen too. It was as if a glass designer had decorated the ceiling.

'What beauty! I feel I can spend my whole life here, admiring this! Can a mere human create such a ceiling? To do that, how many thousand people would need to work for how many years?!' exclaimed Pandian.

'There are millions of invisible sculptors in nature. If we compare with their talent, human sculptors are mere motes,' said the doctor.

Pandian understood that the water seeping from the mud had frozen and formed icicles. But how did so many hues come about? He asked the doctor that question.

'The soil of the Himalayan region is similar to slushy clay. So, the water that percolates here will have many dissolved minerals in it. Each mineral is of a different colour. For instance, the soil that is rich in iron content would be red in colour,' the doctor explained.

They walked within the amazing cave. It seemed like a dream, and they were filled with wonderment. That still cave was filled with peace. The minds of people with deep wisdom are also the same – filled with wonderful things that would be hidden in silence. They can be realized only by people who journey in search of them, who can see that wonderful beauty using their own inner light. Curiosity and humility would be the guiding lamps.

That cave gradually narrowed. Light could be seen at its other end.

On coming out, Pandian saw the peaks first. He felt that his mind had touched the pinnacle too.

Pandian found a song bursting out of him:

Mannum imayamalai engal malaiyae
Maanilam meedhinil idhupoal piridhillaiyae

(The great Himalayan mountains are ours;
And there is none that equal it on this great land!)

'What song is this?' the doctor asked.

'This is also a song by the great poet, Bharathiyar!' Pandian replied.

They walked on the snow. Pandian's heart was elated.

'During the ice ages, a huge river flowed here. In all possibility, it must have been a tributary of the Shivalik River,' said the doctor.

'Ice ages?' queried Pandian.

'Yes. Geologists have discovered that ice ages have occurred several times in the world,' said the doctor.

'What happens during the ice age?' asked Pandian.

'Now, in the current age, thick sheets of ice are found only on poles. At present, they cover only 10 per cent of Earth's surface. If, due to some reason, the temperature of Earth falls, that ice cap would expand. Up to 30 per cent of the land would be covered by ice. That is called "ice age",' the doctor explained.

'How does the temperature of Earth drop?' Pandian could not stop himself from asking questions!

'The surface of Earth is hot due to the sun's rays. If the sunlight reduces, the temperature falls. There can be several reasons for the sunlight to reduce. A long time ago, a huge comet burst in space and shattered into fine dust particles. Those dust particles covered the sky like a huge curtain. Hence, enough sunlight could not reach Earth. In such times, there would be mild sunlight on Earth, only for a few hours each day. That is the reason why an ice age occurred then,' said the doctor.

'When did the last ice age occur?'

'About twelve thousand years ago. At that time, several living creatures on Earth died in the cold. Only those animals that managed to adapt their bodies to the cold managed to live. It appears that this Snowman is one such creature, who came into existence during one such ice age,' the doctor said.

'How?' asked Pandian.

'Millions of years ago, when an ice age occurred, *Ramapithecus* monkey men could have gone extinct, unable to bear the cold. Some monkey men could have discovered the uses of fire. Only they might have survived. Gradually, they evolved into human beings. Some other *Ramapithecus* monkey men may have somehow managed to thrive in the cold and live on the peak of these mountains,' said the doctor.

'The *Ramapithecus* on the peak of the snow mountains adapted their bodies to bear the severe cold. Their sizes became huge and fur grew all over their body to adapt to the cold. Gradually, they evolved into snowmen,' the doctor explained.

'How did they manage to escape and live there?'

'That is a mystery. Their habitats must have some specially adapted features that help them escape the cold.'

'What kind of features?' asked Pandian.

'We can ascertain that only if we go there and see it,' said the doctor.

The next day, they reached the top of a peak. When they stood there, they saw a bizarre scene before them. It was a river of fire!

An Antenna on the Face

What is an important part of the body that animals have but humans do not?

Animals have long hair below their nostrils – vibrissae. They protect the animals' faces. The hair is very fine. Even if a small insect was to sit on their face, these hair would sense it. Immediately the animal would become aware of it.

Why don't humans alone not have it? On a human's face, the hair is not thick like that of animals. The skin on a human's face is very soft. We would become aware even if a speck of dust falls on it. But it is also because of our evolution. We humans became diurnal (active during the day) and began relying heavily on our colour vision. So, we do not need such vibrissae. Hence, gradually it disappeared.

29

Snow stretched out till the horizon. A river of fire was flowing across it.

The doctor said, 'It's a strange river.'

Immediately, Pandian recalled, 'Doctor, this is what the monk had mentioned. This is the river of fire.'

'The monk said that there is a barricade of fire put in by the Buddha around the Dharmasthala where the yetis live,' said Kim.

'I think this is lava. Molten lava that flows out when the earth erupts appears like this, as a river of fire,' said Pandian.

The doctor pulled out the map of that place and looked at it keenly. His face reflected his amazement.

'What, Doctor?' asked Pandian.

'This river of fire is the border between India and Laurasia,' the doctor said. He then pointed at the map. The boundary was marked in it.

'Fascinating!' said Pandian.

'This is the place where the two huge land masses collided – a massive rift.'

They tied the rope and climbed down the steep rock. Then they walked towards the river.

'We can walk on this river of fire,' said the doctor.

'How?' asked Pandian.

'Look there. The snow on the banks has not melted,' the doctor pointed.

They reached the river which glowed red like a huge pit of fire. But, as they neared it, they realized that it was not hot at all!

The doctor bent down. 'Incredible!' he exclaimed.

'What?' asked Pandian.

'These are red diamonds.'

'Diamonds?' Pandian almost shouted.

'True! This is a bed of diamonds,' the doctor said.

Pandian became stupefied. There were heaps and heaps of diamonds!

'How did these diamonds form, Doctor?' asked Pandian.

'There had once been a dense forest here. India's land mass came and collided against it. It hardened gradually. A forest that stretched across several hundred kilometres in breadth crammed together and became the size of a small river. It is the heat and pressure under the earth that converts charcoal into diamonds. This forest got caught in the collision and became charcoal. Due to the pressure from two huge land masses, it gradually became diamonds,' said the doctor.

Pandian's gaze went here and there. The spread of

diamond lay open. Red-coloured light shone from it. 'How many diamonds could there be! Mountains of diamonds! If the world comes to know that there are so many diamonds here, that's it! Everybody in the world will become rich, won't they?' said Pandian.

'That will not happen. Diamonds are usually found under the earth. Only when one digs very deep can they be found. Therefore, as they are discovered only rarely, they have high value. If heaps of diamonds are found, they will lose their value. We might even start using diamonds to build our homes!' said the doctor.

'If we take the diamonds from here, little by little, we can become millionaires,' said Pandian.

'Only if we are able to overcome this desire can we find the Snowman,' said the doctor.

The three of them stepped on the diamonds. This reminded Pandian of the practice of walking on a fire-pit during south Indian temple festivals. In the red glow, he felt as if his entire body was on fire. Pandian thought that fire and diamonds are but the same. There is nothing called fire. Each object has light and heat inside it. When they break out, fire occurs. Fire comes out of wood. Fire comes out of oil. When flints are rubbed, fire comes out. Molten metals become fire. There is fire in the sun. There is fire in the stars. Even under the Earth, there is burning fire. All places and all things are filled with fire. Fire is light! Fire is energy. This is why our ancestors worshipped fire. They considered fire to be a god.

Does man not have fire inside him? Is there not fire in his thoughts? Let the fire inside me erupt! Let my body become light! Let my thoughts become flames! Pandian felt as if his body and mind had gone up in flames, and were burning bright. *All sorts of rubbish get burnt in fire and become ash. Similarly, all my negative thoughts have also burnt and become ash!* thought Pandian.

The three of them reached the other side. Then, Pandian felt that his body and mind had become cleansed. 'Doctor, the indicators mentioned by the monks have all turned out to be accurate. They said that we have to walk on the sea. Then, they said that we have to swim in the fire. Both these things happened right?'

'Therefore, the other details that the monk mentioned should also be correct. It seems that many of them have come here. They have good knowledge of this area,' said the doctor.

They climbed over the glacier. Then, the surface undulated. After some time, they rose again. At last, they reached the rim of a huge mountain. The sight that met them there was spellbinding. On all the four sides, snow clad mountains could be seen. They appeared to be in the shape of a full circle. There was a dense forest in the valley in their midst. The chirping of birds could be heard from there. 'Forest! How did a forest appear here? A forest thriving in the bitter cold of the Himalayan peaks? Unbelievable!' said Pandian.

'There will be a reason for everything,' said the doctor. He keenly observed the mountains through his telescope.

'Doctor, did you notice this? The sun is shining bright between these mountains,' said Pandian.

The doctor smiled and said, 'Yes, I noticed. It is because of the sunshine there that the forests have grown in this altitude.'

'How can the rays of the sun shine only there?' asked Pandian.

'Look at these mountains carefully,' said the doctor.

Pandian keenly observed the mountains through his telescope.

'What can you see?' asked the doctor.

'The slopes of these mountains are curved. They are like the inside of a huge bowl,' said Pandian.

'Yes. These hollow slopes are covered with white snow. That is why these mountain slopes become like enormous concave mirrors,' said the doctor.

'Understood, Doctor. The sunlight that falls on such concave mirrors converges and reflects into this valley. That is why there is more sunlight there,' said Pandian.

'At the peak of the Himalayas, a tropical forest has formed! Is this a game of nature?!' said the doctor.

How Did Coral Lose Its Value?

You would have heard of *navarathinam* – the nine rare gemstones. One among them is diamond, and the other is coral.

In the olden times, coral was found in the sands near the sea. It would be red or yellow in colour. It would be embedded in the ornaments and was also considered very precious, like the diamond.

Then science and technology advanced. It became possible to dive deep into the ocean and undertake research. Only then was it understood what coral actually was. Corals are very tiny animals called polyps.

A long time ago, an ice age occurred. So, the seas became cooler. Immediately, insects across the globe travelled in hordes towards hotter climes. Aren't the places near the equator the hottest? The insects, therefore, went to those places. Adult corals couldn't move. So, they released larvae into the water. The currents carried these larvae with them to hotter places, like near the equator. To protect themselves, the corals secrete a hard skeleton around their soft bodies. Those skeletons are called coral reefs. Then soil got deposited on those rocks. Plants grew on them, they became islands and people began to live on them.

There are many such coral islands to the south of India. Maldives is one such major island.

Today, coral has no value. It has become like a mere pebble. The reason being the abundance in its occurrence.

30

'Doctor, let us go there soon! I am raring to go!'

'Wait! It is an even bigger forest than we're assuming,' said the doctor.

They reached the rim of the peak and looked to see whether there was a way to go down.

'Now I am able to understand how this place was formed,' said the doctor.

'How?'

'It is the crater of a huge volcano.'

'Volcano?'

'Yes. This is an extinct ancient volcano. Several million years ago, there were thousands of volcanoes like this on Earth. The molten lava that gushed out of them has hardened to form many of the mountains that we see today.'

'How do you know that this is the mouth of a volcano?' Pandian asked.

'Look at these mountains. They are nice and round in shape. The inner slope is hollow. The outer side is rugged,' said the doctor.

'Yes, Doctor. This is like the hollow that forms on the top of a lighted candle. These mountains are like the solidified molten wax that drips to the sides.'

They pondered on how to climb down. The inner slopes of the mountains were curved inwards. Hence, they were not able to climb down like they usually would do in mountains.

'Come, let us walk around and check. Some path might open to us.'

At one spot, snow cascaded down in waves. Each wave was like a step.

'The snow from the top of the mountain melted, flowed down and then became hard again. This is how these snow steps are formed,' said the doctor.

They went down the steps. It was an easy descent. At one place, the snow started becoming softer. Then, it became like ice cream.

'We cannot go down further. We will get buried in the snow,' said Pandian.

'Come. It is dangerous to stand on the snow now,' said the doctor.

By that time, the snowy ground on which they had been standing cracked and split open. They screamed in fear and began to fall down fast. That snowy slope suddenly became a huge river. Dashing over the rocks, the river flowed down the mountain like a huge waterfall. The currents tossed and dragged them along. Their vehicle also got pulled in the current. At one point, that huge river tumbled down the sheer surface of a tall rock. That sound was deafening. Water droplets misted over the fall like thick smoke.

Pandian understood that if they were to fall down from that, death would be inevitable. The place where water falls down from a great height is very dangerous. Anything that fell with the water would get dragged into greater depths by the speed of the currents. As water would keep falling on top, it would not be possible to swim to the surface. Only after swimming underwater for a long distance can one come up to the surface. By that time, while one is straining for breath, life will have ebbed out.

Pandian caught hold of a rock immediately. The other rocks were rounded and slippery as water was continuously falling on them. They could not be grabbed. But this rock alone was split – possibly due to some other rock dragged by the current dashing against it. The edge of that split rock was very sharp. It cut into his hand. Pandian was in great pain. But he did not let go of his hold. The doctor caught hold of Pandian's legs. Kim grabbed the doctor's legs. The three of them together were quite heavy. That weight dragged Pandian's hands. He felt that his hand would be ripped apart. Still, he did not let go of his grip.

Kim climbed up, holding onto the doctor's hands. He climbed with the agility of a garden lizard climbing a tree, and reached the rock. The doctor too climbed over Pandian's body and reached the rock. Lastly, both of them together pulled up Pandian. He got onto the top too.

Blood oozed out of his palms. It was as if his palms had been split open with a sickle.

'It is a deep cut indeed. But the blood vessels have constricted as cold water has fallen over it. There will not be much blood loss,' said the doctor.

When they looked around, they could see several streams falling from all sides of the mountains. Those streams looked like white towels hung out to dry from a clothesline. They flapped and furled from the mountain.

'This valley is hot. That is the reason why snow from the peak melts and flows down,' said the doctor.

'The cold has decreased,' observed Pandian.

'There are no snowbanks ahead. We can climb down through the rocks,' said the doctor.

They began to climb down. The rocks were wet with moss. Their hands and legs slipped. Deep down below, the tops of trees could be seen.

'If we lose our grip, rescuers might not even get our bones!' said Pandian.

'We must focus only on our hands and legs. Lord Buddha will take care of the rest,' said Kim.

They climbed down amid the rocks. As they descended, they felt the heat of that place. There were several birds on the trees below. Squawking, they scattered. One bird among them flapped its wings and came flying up. It came near them and rested on a rock.

'Ah! This is not a bird. This is a flying lizard,' exclaimed Pandian.

'Yes. Its name is *Archaeopteryx*. It belongs to the dinosaur family,' said the doctor.

The lizard-bird gave a terrible squawk and flapped its wings.

'Dinosaur family?' said Pandian.

'Yes. Once upon a time, dinosaurs lived and were spread all over the world. That is called the Jurassic Age. That was approximately about 180 million years ago. There were several types of dinosaurs. There were dinosaurs ten times bigger than an elephant. There were dinosaurs that were the size of a small garden lizard too. Our common lizard, monitor lizard, ant-eater, are all part of the dinosaur family. This one here is still surviving, though it is supposed to be extinct. Really surprising!' said the doctor.

The lizard-bird flew away.

'This is a strange land. It appears that evolution has not happened here in the last 150 million years. Many more such amazing creatures could probably exist here,' said the doctor.

Flying Dinosaur

An archaeological excavation took place near the town of Solnhofen in Germany. There, under the earth, set in a limestone rock, the fossil of a bird's bones was unearthed.

When the skeleton was examined, it was found to be that of a strange bird. It had the claws on all three of its fingers. It had a big jaw and also many teeth in its mouth. It had scales on its body. It had a long tail. At the same time, it was a bird too.

The skeletal structure of that bird was similar to that of a Theropod dinosaur. That bird is a cross between birds and dinosaurs. Scientists have named it *Archaeopteryx*.

31

Pandian climbed down the rocks carefully. A huge tree stood below. He directly stepped down on the branches of that tree. Then, Kim and the doctor got down on the treetop. From their vantage point at the top, it had appeared to be a dense forest full of trees. Only after coming down did they appreciate how big a jungle it was!

Each tree that stood there was enormous. The branches of the trees were as thick as the trunks of the biggest trees back in our towns. Many types of creepers were found densely entwined with those trees. Pandian sat on that tree and peered down. He could see only dense foliage. The jungle floor could not be seen at all! The trees could be climbed easily hanging on to the creepers.

'You did notice how many rivers empty into this valley as waterfalls, didn't you? As the water is abundant, the jungle has grown dense,' said the doctor.

'If an area is kept hidden from human eyes, dense forests will grow there automatically. But if a road is laid in this place, that would be enough! People will immediately bring their lorries. They will start felling trees and selling them. In ten years, there will be no trees left in this place,' said Pandian.

'Yes. It is man's avarice that has destroyed the jungles of Earth. As the forest cover gradually decreased, the fertility of the soil declined. Rainfall decreased too and as a result, the yield from farms reduced too.'

They felt hungry. Several ripe fruits hung on the branches of the tree and the creepers. But the doctor and Pandian hesitated to eat them. Kim had no such misgivings. 'Doctor! Did the monk not refer to this place as Dharmasthala? All the fruits here are like divine nectar. We can eat anything,' he said.

Then he plucked a fruit and started eating it. Pandian also plucked a fruit and began to eat it. It was not like a fruit at all. It was like a sweet cake!

'This fruit is high in natural sugar content. That is why it tastes like this,' said the doctor.

After eating the fruits, Kim climbed up the tree and went higher. The foliage was dense and creepers wove thickly amid the leaves. Hence, it provided a net-like canopy. Kim lay down on the leafy hammock. It was like sleeping on a comfortable mattress. Sun shone pleasantly there.

Pandian and the doctor too laid down similarly. Pandian removed his clothes and the doctor did the same. Their skin was very pale. When the sun's rays touched them, they felt the heat intensely.

'Sunlight and air are very essential for our skin. Our pigment cells will die if not exposed to sunlight. Hence the health of the skin reduces,' said the doctor.

The three of them fell asleep talking.

Pandian woke up with a start on hearing a scraping noise.

An animal stood near him. He first thought that it was a horse, but its neck was short. The legs were like that of a monkey. Holding on to the tree with its toes, it grazed on the leaves.

The doctor woke up too. He observed the animal closely.

'Doctor, is this a monkey or a horse?' asked Pandian.

'Definitely a horse. All the creatures here are at the stage where they have not yet evolved into the beings we know. Several million years ago, horses were like this. There were five toes on their legs. They used to climb on trees and live eating its leaves,' said the doctor.

'How did they get hooves on their legs then?' asked Pandian.

'Hooves are just nails. The trees in the jungle began to decrease and the land became increasingly filled with grass. Horses began to live on grasslands. Hence, they needed to run long distances. To run fast, they exerted pressure on only one toe. The nail on that toe became thick and formed the hoof.'

'But isn't a horse's neck long?' asked Pandian.

'Yes. When the horse began to run fast, its legs grew longer. And to compensate it, its neck became longer too. Only then could it bend down and graze, isn't it?' the doctor said.

Pandian observed the horse keenly. It flicked its tail about and tossed its mane. But it jumped from tree to tree like a monkey! If these horses were trained, one could journey across trees. If, in the city of Chennai, one were to ride on this, one could even climb on and jump between tall buildings like a monkey! Pandian laughed at the mental image.

Meanwhile, several horses began to gather. They wandered on the trees, grazing.

'I am eager to see the other animals here,' said Pandian.

How Did the Horse Evolve?

Vladimir Kovalevsky was a Russian zoologist who had researched the evolutionary history of horses.

A fossil of an animal that had lived 50 million years ago was found. It had four toes on its front feet and three toes on its back feet. That was the predecessor of the horse. Its name is *Eohippus*.

Later, this creature began to live on grasslands. It evolved into an animal called *Mesohippus*, with long legs.

Then, the neck of that animal became longer. It is called *Pliohippus*.

Lastly, the horse that we see today evolved. It is called by the Latin name, *Equus*.

32

Still grazing, those horses wandered away.

'These horses do not face scarcity of food here. Look how plump they are!' said Pandian, staring with his mouth agape.

Kim said, 'Look, down there … cows!'

The three of them peered down. On the ground, herds of cows the size of elephants were moving about. Their horns were very long and curved.

'Look at their legs. They are the legs of a monkey! There is no soil to be seen anywhere here. The floor is possibly covered by broken branches. Several types of shrubs have grown densely over them. Only when the legs have a grip like that of a monkey can one walk here,' said the doctor.

The top of the trees also had a dense canopy of leaves and creepers like the one that covered the forest floor. Kim placed his leg on it. The leg got a little buried, but he did not fall down or slip.

'Doctor, I am able to walk well,' said Kim.

Pandian too tried to walk. It felt as if he was walking on hay. The three of them ran across it. They could run easily while swaying from side to side.

There were several varieties of birds on the trees. Green coloured crows flew about cawing! An unusual sparrow drew their attention. When it was on the branches, it was green in colour. When it rose in flight, it turned light blue. Pandian pounced and caught hold of a parrot. That parrot had no colour at all. It was transparent, as if made of glass. One could see the other side through its body.

'How strange!' exclaimed Pandian.

Several types of green- and red-coloured sparrows flew about. Some sparrows had wide jaws like that of a lizard. There were teeth inside the mouth too. Then they saw red-coloured peacocks screeching. The male peacock spread out its feathers. It was fantastic to see red-coloured peacock feathers.

Pandian suddenly noticed a bird and exclaimed, 'Doctor, look there!'

The bird that he pointed out had a long body. It had four wings. It was like a very big butterfly. Its wings were light red in colour.

'Are the creatures here insects or lizards or birds? I am not able to discern,' said Pandian.

'These three species are closely related to each other. If we were to compare the skeleton of a bird with that of a lizard, there would only be very few noticeable differences. The forelegs of the lizards gradually became wings,' explained the doctor.

Just then, a bird flew, crossing them. Pandian said, 'Aha! A flying fish!'

The bird that flew by was just like a swordfish. There were silver scales on its body. Its fins had grown big to become wings. Its mouth was open. There were several teeth inside it. But the tip of its nose was long like a beak.

'In the course of evolution, fishes have become birds too. All creatures are connected to each other,' said the doctor.

Then, they went on, observing the multitude of strange creatures around them. They saw squirrels with wings. They saw lizards with cat-like faces that stuck onto the trees. In one place, a large number of dogs pranced about, hopping on trees. They had horns like that of goats. Their legs were like those of monkeys too. They saw a very big spider. Using its forelegs, the spider plucked a coconut-like fruit. Breaking the fruit open, it picked up the pieces and ate them. There were several fishes on another tree; they had legs like that of crabs. They climbed up the branches using their legs to hold onto them. They saw several types of snakes. On seeing them, a snake raised its hood, which then spread wide outwards and became a wing. Rising, it flew away. They saw multi-hued insects that appeared like glass globules flying about. They saw pigs, seated, holding on to the branches with their small legs.

They were stunned on seeing a particular animal. It was a buffalo, but it had a total of eight legs. Those legs were cramped, like those of a crocodile. Three toes with sharp nails could be seen on each leg. That buffalo-like creature climbed the trees and grazed on the leaves. On seeing them, it tossed its horns and grunted just like a buffalo. Two small calves, just like it, could be seen near it.

Then, they saw an even stranger creature. It was a python, but it had several small legs on both sides of its body like a millipede. Moving those legs along, it crawled on the branches.

They then saw something even weirder. It was a very big crab! While the creature's legs were like that of a crab, its head was like that of a cow. There were even two horns on that head. It kept chewing cud like a cow. On seeing them, it bleated like a cow.

'Is this real or a dream? I am not able to fathom,' said Pandian.

'This is Lord Buddha's painting hall. He draws in different ways,' said Kim.

'Don't blabber,' said Pandian.

'What he says is true. Nature creates different characteristics. In the course of evolution, only whichever feature is superior and useful continues. The ones that are not, die out. These are the creatures that have become extinct over time,' said the doctor.

Just then, they saw an even weirder creature.

Flying Animals

A particular type of squirrel species in Africa can fly! When they jump between the trees, their legs spread very wide. Then, the skin near the legs stretches out. Hence, they fly like a kite and land safely on the ground.

In Sri Lanka and East Indian islands, there is a creature called Cajuan. It looks like a squirrel. It is also an animal with the ability to fly. This is a big creature, approximately the size of a big cat. The animal 'phalanger', that lives in the Philippines, is like a kangaroo. There is a pouch in its stomach too. It keeps its young one inside it. It jumps from tall trees. Like a kite, it lands safely on the ground.

33

On seeing the creature, Pandian initially stood stupefied. Then he burst out into huge guffaws. It looked as if several kinds of animals had been bashed together. Its hands and legs were like that of a monkey, while its face was like a fox. It had goat's horns but a tail like that of a garden lizard. That creature sat on a branch, sunning itself happily. It turned on hearing Pandian's laughter and said, 'Miaow.'

Pandian could not control his laughter.

'There is nothing to laugh about, Pandian. Do you know what the first car developed by Henry Ford looked like? It would be like a chariot but fitted with bicycle tires! If one were to look at that car after seeing today's cars, one would feel like laughing. But it is from that car that today's car has evolved. Evolution too happens thus,' said the doctor.

That creature ran away with another 'miaow'.

They saw a few more similar, weird creatures.

'If I continue to see some more animals like this, I will go mad,' said Pandian.

Kim, who had been silent till then, began to speak. 'In the paintings on the walls of our monastery, weird forms like these are depicted. These are the animals that would come along with Lord Buddha when he would be reborn.'

'Lord Buddha would be born again?' Pandian asked, confounded.

'Such a belief exists in the Buddhist religion. The Bodhisattva, who would be born again, would be known by the name Maitreyar,' said the doctor.

'Why would he be born again?' asked Pandian.

'When evil takes over, the world as we know it will get destroyed. Then, Maitreyar will create a new world. Kim claims that these creatures would come along with him then,' the doctor explained.

'That monk we met earlier too claimed that after an apocalypse, Snowmen would spread all over the world,' said Pandian.

'Yes,' agreed the doctor.

'If that be so, when Maitreyar is reborn, would the snowmen and these creatures populate Earth?' Pandian asked.

'Yes. There is a subtle mystery in this which we are not able to comprehend,' said the doctor.

'Where is the Snowman? We have not seen him till now!' said Pandian.

'We have not seen them but the yetis are watching us,' said Kim.

'Yes. I sense that too. Snowmen have a very highly evolved consciousness. They would already know that we are approaching this jungle. I am unable to ascertain how they are aware of this, but they definitely know it. They have saved us from dangers. They lifted and moved our tent from the base of that snow mountain,' the doctor said.

'Why would they save us?' asked Pandian.

'They like us coming here. Anyone whom they do not like cannot enter this area,' said the doctor.

'Why? Why do they want us to come here?' Pandian did not stop his relentless questioning.

'I do not know whether they want all the three of us or just one among us,' the doctor said.

Just then, the Snowman appeared in front of them. He rose from atop a tree. He stood silent.

Pandian got scared. 'Doctor, now I understand. He planned and helped us to come here so he could capture us. We are really trapped!' He yelled and pulled out his revolver. He aimed at the Snowman.

The Snowman walked slowly towards them. He was not afraid of the gun. Pandian pressed the trigger. At that very instant, he felt as if somebody had tugged his hand away. The bullet missed and went off the mark. Pandian tried shooting again but he could not move his hand at all. His hands became heavy and felt lifeless. The gun fell down as he lost his grip. Immediately, he felt life returning to his hands.

The Snowman came near. He was very tall. His body was covered thickly with ash-coloured hair. It seemed as soft and thick as that of a Pomeranian. He did not stumble even a little when he walked over the leaves. Pandian immediately noticed his legs. They were like that of a monkey! He walked with his feet slightly turned out.

Pandian recollected seeing the photograph of the Snowman's footprints for the first time. On that day, he had noticed that the feet were turned out. From that, he had inferred that the Snowman was a monkey. Now, he understood that the Snowman was not really a monkey. Only his hands and legs were like a monkey's – and Pandian realized it was so because the Snowman lived on the trees.

The Snowman then came near them.

A Fish That Walks

Do you know what is a Stegocephalus? It was an archaic life form.

Its bones have been fossilised on ancient coral reefs. This creature had a lung. It had legs like that of a lizard. Five toes could be seen on those legs. But it was a fish! Yes. Several million years ago, fishes that climbed to the shore and walked around lived!

34

As the Snowman neared them, Kim fell to his knees. He prostrated before the Snowman as per the Buddhist traditions. His hands touched Kim's head.

Then, the Snowman said something. That voice had a beautiful cadence. It was as if a big tanpura was being played.

'Did you notice how Kim prostrated before the Snowman? Buddhists bow like this only before their gurus,' said the doctor.

Surprised, Pandian asked, 'Is that so?'

Kim got up. The Snowman raised both his hands. Immediately, from all directions, the voices of several snow people were heard. It sounded as if several musical instruments were being played together in perfect harmony. A large number of snow people rose from the trees. There were women and children among them. With joyful squeals they moved towards the three people.

As they chittered joyfully, Pandian observed something different. When animals make a noise or birds raise their calls, it would be a screeching rancour. It would be the same when several humans talk at once. Each and every animal, bird and human would make a separate sound. When such sounds come together, they would only create a discordant noise. But, when insects make a noise, this is not the case. Even if there are tens of millions of insects that make noise, it would sound melodious. They would start and stop in sync. Pandian noticed that the sounds made by the snow people too were in sync. Even when so many of them talked, it sounded like one voice. Pandian could not contain his astonishment.

The snow people came running and lifted them up. The little children of the snowmen pranced about. Unable to control their excitement, they jumped up and down.

'How happy are they to see us!' The doctor said, amazed.

'How did I think badly of them!' said Pandian.

The snow people lifted and carried them.

A big meadow could be seen; it was green. There were many snow people there. But it was not flat ground. It was the top portion of a dense forest. Several cows grazed among the snow people.

They put the three men down. Snow children gave them various kinds of fruits. Then, the snow people pranced about in the sun like how fishes jump about, playing in the water.

As the sun slowly set, the surrounding snowy peaks turned yellow at first. Then they became red. Then, they turned a deeper red. One by one, the snow people gathered and sat down, facing the west. Within a short time, a large number of them had gathered there.

'There are definitely at least three thousand snow people here,' estimated the doctor.

All of them sat facing the setting sun. The sunlight spread over their faces and they glowed red. Very quietly, they began to sing. It was actually not a song – they were just humming. But all of them hummed in one voice. There was not a single discordant note. It felt as if three thousand musicians were playing three thousand violins together, without even a single note out of place.

Kim slowly went and sat near them. He turned his eyes towards the sun. Slowly he began to hum too.

'Doctor! Let us join them too! What spellbinding music! We would not be able to listen to such amazing music again in our life,' said Pandian.

'Yes,' agreed the doctor. They too went and sat there.

That music was enthralling. It rose, fell and twirled in a lilting cadence. But Pandian was not able to participate in that music. He could not concentrate on it enough. He hummed with the music for some time. Suddenly, he would be reminded of something. Consequently, he would be reminded of some other thing. Then, he would remember the music again. Immediately he would join in the humming. But then his mind wandered again.

How much ever he tried, Pandian could not hum along continuously. So, he stopped humming and simply listened to it. The doctor was detached from the music too. But Kim became completely one with the music; he had also become one with the snow people.

Gradually, the darkness grew denser around them. The snow people laid down where they were and went to sleep. Kim too laid down with them and went to sleep.

The doctor and Pandian laid down too.

'I am not able to understand what is happening,' said Pandian.

'Did you notice the snow people making a single sound like insects?' asked the doctor.

'Yes,' said Pandian.

'In a manner of speaking, they are like insects too. Animals, birds and humans have separate minds of their own. But insects do not. They only have a hive mind and intuition. That intuition is the same for all the insects,' said the doctor.

'What about these snow people, then?' asked Pandian.

'I am not able to fathom. But, all their minds have together become one single mind,' said the doctor.

'How? It is really amazing,' said Pandian.

'Consider we have someone really close to us. Assume that we both share a deep bond of affection and love. We could see that sometimes, they would have the same thoughts as us,' the doctor said.

'True, Doctor. At school, I had a very close friend. His name was Balu. At times I would think of something. By the time I would say it, he would say the very same thing himself,' said Pandian.

'Exactly! At that time, both your minds had become one. In the same manner, the minds of all these snow people have become one,' said the doctor.

'How come, Doctor? I am unable to wrap my head around it!'

'I am not able to comprehend this, either. Let us ask Kim when he wakes up tomorrow morning!'

Plants That Evolve

Russian evolutionary biologist Kliment Timiryazev performed an experiment. He took a thorny plant that was native to the deserts of Jerusalem. It had a thick stem, its leaves were dense and it would grow tall.

He transplanted that plant on the top of a hill. It was colder there. So, the growth of that plant also stunted. Its leaves spread sidewards. That is, the plant developed the characteristics needed to thrive in the cold. The various plants all around the world have been through such evolutions to adapt to their habitats.

35

Lying on their backs, they gazed up at the sky. Pandian looked at the stars in amazement. The stars were pale blue in colour. They appeared to be very close to them, nearer than usual. Huge blue-hued fireflies rose in swarms and flew by. Each firefly was the size of a zero-watt bulb. They looked like flying stars. After a while, a different type of firefly came in droves. They were red-hued while their light was blue in colour.

Pandian caught a blue-coloured firefly that had landed on him. It was the same insect that they had seen in the morning. A blue light could be seen inside its body.

'This is the same swordfish that we saw today morning,' the doctor said, pointing at another point of light.

Then, many more such colourful fireflies rose in hordes. They eventually realized that the yellow-hued fireflies were actually flying garden lizards. The skin under their stomach lit up with a yellow light. The green-hued ones were actually a type of sparrow. Though they were shining with bright light now, they were merely unattractive brown sparrows during the day. Then, slowly, they drifted off to sleep.

In the morning, the early rays of the sun touched them. Immediately, they opened their eyes.

Kim and the snow people were not to be seen anywhere.

'Where did they go?' wondered the doctor.

Then, a snow child came running towards them. Laughing, the child said in Ladakhi language, 'Come, let us go for a bath!'

Pandian exclaimed in surprise, 'This snow child speaks Ladakhi!'

'I am surprised too!' agreed the doctor.

They ran behind the child.

Running across tree-tops, they reached the wide bank of a river. It was a very broad river. In it, blue-coloured water swirled in waves. They realized that the river was very deep. Several snow people were bathing in that river. They dipped in and out of water, and also splashed in it, looking like they were having fun.

'Come, let us bathe,' said Pandian.

Both of them removed their dresses. They slowly stepped down into the water. The water was comfortably warm. They saw a boulder in front of them. Standing on the rock, some snow children were frolicking about. Pandian swam towards the rock.

Pandian noticed Kim standing on that rock along with the snow children. Like the snow people, Kim, too, did not wear any clothes at all. He romped about with the snow children.

Suddenly, that boulder sank into the river. The children squealed in delight as they fell into the water. In the distance, the boulder came up again.

It was not a rock. It was an enormous tortoise! Pandian looked at it in amazement. It was then that he realized that the many 'boulders' in that river were actually huge tortoises.

A big tortoise came swimming towards them. A snowman was standing on it. He said, 'Climb onto this.'

Pandian went near the gargantuan tortoise. Its legs were like the trunks of a huge tree. Scales like those of a crocodile could be seen on them. Using those scales as footholds, Pandian climbed up.

Once he was up on the tortoise, the Snowman said, 'There is absolutely no need for you to fear anything here.'

'How do you know the Ladakhi language?' Pandian asked.

'Ladakhi language? I do not know anything like that. I wanted to talk to you, and this kind of speech comes to me. I do not know what language this is,' said the Snowman.

Then, huge waves rose in the water near them. A gigantic lion-face rose from the water. There were two huge eyes on that lion's face. Its nose was broad. Its maw was open. White teeth were seen inside its mouth. Between the rows of teeth, a long, red-coloured tongue could be seen. However, the lion did not have a mane. It gave a ferocious roar.

Pandian wondered how a lion could live in the water. Only the lion's head could be seen above the surface now, like a big boulder.

The lion's head rose slowly. Then its body came out of the water – it was like that of a snake. But it had four legs like a crocodile. Those legs did not have any toes; instead, they had huge webs like the ones seen on a duck's feet. That creature paddled and swam on the water. It was fascinating to see it coming out of the water. It was similar to the small trains for children that could be found in parks!

Pandian sensed that he had seen that creature somewhere.

What Is Civilization?

Around 200 years ago, David Livingstone, a Scotsman, reached Africa. He referred to Africa as the 'Dark Continent'. Europeans claim that it was he who 'discovered' Africa.

But humans had lived for thousands of years already in the continent. They had lived in harmony and joy.

Some white people shot at and killed Africans with their guns. They captured those people, put them in ships and took them to America. There, they sold them like cattle. The Africans were put in chains and made to work. They were kept as slaves. The children born to them were kept as slaves too.

Who are civilized? Africans or those white men?

36

The weird creature with the head of a lion and the tail of a snake swam fast in the water. Suddenly, it turned its head back and let out a hiss, just like a snake. It appeared as if steam was coming out through its nostrils.

Pandian then realized what that creature was – it was a dragon! In China and Japan, there are numerous paintings of this creature. During festivals, Chinese make giant cloth puppets of such a dragon. Seven or eight people dance, lifting it. It would appear as if the dragon was dancing. But the dragon is an imaginary creature. It is a mythical creature from ancient lore. That was how he had thought till now. Here, a real dragon was playing and swimming in the water.

This meant that dragons would have lived in China a long time ago. Then, they would have become extinct later. Only stories about them have survived. The people who came later thought they were a mere figment of imagination. As per ancient lore, a dragon would spit fire from its nostrils. Now, Pandian understood why. The steam that arises from the dragon's nostrils was thought to be smoke from a fire.

The children of the snow people jumped on the dragon. They hung from the hairs on the dragon's tail. Each hair was as heavy as a rope. Pandian grabbed hold of a hair too. The dragon plunged into the water. The depths of the water were pale blue in colour. In the blue expanse, tiny lightning-like rays could be seen.

The dragon plunged into the depths. It kept going deeper and deeper into the water. Differently coloured, peculiar fishes were gliding by. The dragon went deeper still. The bottom of the river could be seen. The riverbed was made of yellow-coloured stones. Pandian observed them keenly – they sparkled, emitting a shining light. He could touch them. Immediately, Pandian picked one up.

The dragon rose to the surface quickly. Pandian took in a deep breath. The dragon breathed in deeply too. Pandian realized that, just like humans, the dragon could also only breathe outside the water.

Pandian climbed onto another tortoise. He looked at the pebble in his hand. It was a block of gold! Pandian was filled with wonderment. The bottom of that river was filled with rocks of gold. There were mountains of gold there!

The snow people began to climb up onto the shore. Pandian felt very hungry. He too swam and climbed ashore. When he reached the shore, a snowman lifted him up. He swung him around and flung him afar.

Pandian soared high in the air and landed on the trees. He felt as if he were falling on a haystack.

There, snow people were plucking fruits and eating them. The fruits were like sweet coconuts. The sun was shining hot there. He became dry by the time he had finished eating.

The doctor came near Pandian.

'What's up, Pandian? Did you have a good bath?' he asked.

'Yes, Doctor. Here, have a look at this,' said Pandian. He showed the chunk of gold to the doctor.

'I noticed too. There are several rocks of gold here. The bottom of the river is full of gold. Pure gold,' said the doctor.

'Gold is not found separately anywhere, isn't it? It would always be found in ores, or alloyed with some other metal or mixed in the soil, right?' queried Pandian.

'Have you forgotten that we are now inside the mouth of a volcano? Gold might have become isolated due to the heat from the volcano.'

At that moment, the snow children went running past them. Kim ran along with them too. With a pounce, Pandian grabbed him.

At first, Kim did not recognize them at all. Eyes wide open, he stared at them as if he had just woken up from a deep sleep.

'Look here, Kim,' said the doctor.

Kim roused himself. 'Doctor Saab!' he said.

'What happened to you? Why are you staring like this?' asked Pandian.

'I went and sat with the yetis yesterday evening. I heard their music. I too hummed along with them. I do not remember anything after that,' said Kim.

'What happened? Try to make an effort and recollect,' the doctor urged.

'It was as if I was in a big dream. It was a long dream,' said Kim.

'What?' asked the doctor.

'In that dream, I could do a number of things all at once. I was in the forest. I ate fruits. I frolicked in the river. I played, I flew in the sky. I got stuck with the plants. I pierced the fruits and entered them. It was me who was spread under the soil.'

'It seems to be such a strange dream?' said Pandian.

'Tell me more,' insisted the doctor.

'I then felt that there was nothing that I could not do. I also felt that there was nothing that I did not know,' said Kim.

'Alright, you may go now,' said the doctor.

Kim ran off.

'What is this? He is rambling as if he's mad?' Pandian asked.

'Now I understand how the minds of the snow people work,' said the doctor.

'How?' asked Pandian.

'I will explain. I now understand how they came to know Ladakhi too,' said the doctor.

Mexico's Mountains of Gold

In the olden days, plenty of gold was available in Mexico. So, the Aztec people who lived there held it in little value. They treated it like rocks and soil. The reason being that they had no use for it.

In 1519, a sailor called Cortez came to Mexico from Spain. He came there, as he had heard that lot of gold was available in Mexico. The Aztec people understood that he had travelled that far only for gold. They gave him a mound of gold as high as the wheel of a bullock cart.

On seeing that, Cortez was filled with avarice. He killed the Aztec people and captured Mexico.

For 300 continuous years after that, Spain plundered Mexico's gold. Millions of people were killed for that.

37

'How does a snowperson's mind work?' asked Pandian.

'What do we refer to when we say "mind"?' asked the doctor.

'Thoughts keep coming into our minds at all times. Whatever we do, wherever we go, those thoughts do not stop. We call that flow of thoughts our mind.'

'Without you revealing them, can others become aware of your thoughts?'

'No.'

'So, those thoughts belong only to you. That is your mind, isn't it?'

'Yes,' said Pandian.

'The one to which we refer as our mind is just the surface level of our consciousness. There are other minds even deeper,' said the doctor.

'Is that so?'

'Think about this – you read a book ten years back. Then, you forgot about it. Now, suddenly you remember it. So, where was it all this time?

'I do not know.'

'It was within you, right? It was hidden somewhere. That is, you have another mind within you that you are not aware of. That is the subconscious mind.'

'It's truly amazing,' said Pandian.

'There is a super-conscious mind even deeper. Normally, we are not even aware of it.'

'Can we not know it at all?'

'We cannot be aware of it completely. Our dreams all come from this super-conscious mind only.'

'Yes, Doctor. Sometimes, things that I do not even know about, come in my dreams,' admitted Pandian.

'Yes. The super-conscious mind does not belong to just one person. It is spread among all humans. It is the conscious mind that is separate for each individual,' said the doctor.

'That is, for all human beings like you and me, there is only one super-conscious mind, right?'

'Yes. Small creatures have only the super-conscious mind. They do not have separate conscious minds of their own. Only if you articulate can other people be aware of the thoughts in your conscious mind. But insects do not have a conscious mind. So, they all think alike. There is no need to talk.'

'I understood, Doctor! These snow people are the same, right? They do not have conscious minds either. There is only one mind for all of them together. So, there is no need for them to talk among themselves. They think and act in unison, don't they?

'Yes. That is why all of them are able to speak as one voice at the same time. Only insects can hum like that,' said the doctor.

Just then a loud trumpeting noise was heard. Below their feet, they could feel tremors as if a horde of animals were stampeding.

The doctor immediately climbed down from the treetops. Pandian descended too. Beneath the trees, in the forest, massive elephants lumbered by. Their bodies were heavily covered with thick, black hair. Their tusks were very long and curved. Those elephants were five times bigger than the normal elephants.

'Doctor, are these elephants?' asked Pandian.

'They belong to the elephant family. These are the ancient elephants who lived in the snow age. They are called mammoths. Complete mammoth skeletons were discovered,' said the doctor.

'But its legs are different, aren't they? They are like the legs of dinosaurs,' said Pandian.

Three enormous toes could be seen on the mammoth's legs. There were huge nails on those toes.

'It appears that such legs are needed to walk around in these forests,' said the doctor.

The path through which the mammoths were going could be ascertained by the movement of treetops.

'We still haven't had a look at this forest fully. If snow people were to help us, we could explore better.'

'Let us simply ask them, now that they even know Ladakhi,' said Pandian.

Just then, two planes came flying towards them. They were black in colour. They were glider planes did could soar across the sky. Only when they came nearer that the men realize that they were not planes but very big birds! They swooped down and landed. When they folded their wings, it was obvious that they were enormous bats.

A snow child was sitting astride one bat. The child jumped down and said to the doctor, 'You wanted to explore the forest. That is why I brought them. You can get on them and fly around.'

'How do you know what we thought of just now?' asked Pandian.

'We know. What is so astonishing about it?' the snow child asked.

They both sat on the bats.

'How do we ride them? asked Pandian.

They held tightly onto the folds of the skin at the bat's neck. Pandian wanted to fly. Even before he said it aloud, the bat began to rise up and fly. The bat on which the doctor sat flew along too.

Riding on the bat felt like flying on a glider plane.

A glider plane is like a huge kite. There would be very small machinery inside it. A flyer would have to tie themselves to the plane. The glider would then soar like a kite and begin to glide down. Immediately the machinery would be started. The glider would then begin to fly. The experience would be similar to that of flying while holding on to a kite.

But there was a unique difference while flying on the bat. Glider planes have to be directed and turned using hands, legs and machinery. But the bat would turn the moment one thought of turning! Pandian wanted to go down. The bat swooped down. The forest below was dense. In its middle, just like the centre parting of hair, a river could be seen flowing.

Father of Psychology

Sigmund Freud was an Austrian philosopher. He discovered that a human mind has three levels. What we normally refer to as our mind is just the surface level. He called this the conscious mind.

The one expressed in our dreams is our deeper mind. It is made up of thoughts that we have forgotten. Freud called this the subconscious mind.

All human minds are deeply personal and private. We can refer to it as the deeper mind. Freud calls it the unconscious mind.

Freud is called the father of modern psychology.

38

Sitting on the bat, Pandian flew over the forest. Only then did he realize how huge that jungle was. Wherever he turned, he saw dense thickets of trees. There were several varieties of trees. On the tree-tops, different species of birds and animals lived in groups.

One can never finish exploring the animals and birds here. There are several thousands of birds and animals here, Pandian thought.

Pandian noticed a peculiar small bird flying near him. It was a mosquito, but it was as big as a sparrow. Pandian saw that mosquito sitting on a fruit and sucking its juice. On the riverbanks, a spread of golden-coloured slush could be seen. Pandian thought that perhaps they could land there to take a closer look. Immediately, the bat swooped and landed there. The doctor too landed near him.

The bats left them and flew away.

'The moment we wish to go back, they will return,' reassured the doctor.

Thick, heavy slush could be seen on the riverbank. In that mud, several rabbit-sized small creatures frisked and frolicked about.

'Bandicoots?' asked Pandian.

'Aha!' cried the doctor.

Pandian looked at them carefully. He was stumped! The reason being that those creatures were elephants! They had trunks and legs just like that of elephants. A few even had tusks. They resembled elephants exactly.

'They are like toy elephants!' said Pandian.

Pandian lifted one elephant. It wriggled like a rabbit and butted him with its small forehead. Lifting its trunk, it trumpeted. The sound was very soft.

'It has become frightened. Put it down,' said the doctor.

Pandian set that elephant down. Twirling its little tail, it ran off to join the other elephants. Flapping their ears, the elephants played in the mud in groups. A few elephants were swimming about and playing in the water.

The doctor sat on a rock. Pandian sat down on another rock.

'I am not able to understand whatever is happening here. How do the snow people know of everything that we think?' asked Pandian.

'Our bodies have evolved over several million years. Similarly, our minds would have evolved too, right?' asked the doctor.

'Yes. If that is so, then in ancient times, did all humans have only one mind like the snow people do now? asked Pandian.

'Possibly. Simple creatures like insects that have not undergone the evolutionary phases have one mind. Our individual minds would have gradually evolved within us ...' the doctor continued. 'Scientists have conducted research on several tribal populations that have not undergone modernization and civilization. There is no word for "me" in their language. The reason is they do not consider themselves as separate.'

'How did that individual identity evolve in humans, then?' asked Pandian.

'Several million years ago, humans lived in groups. At that time, they did not have the identity of "I". Later, they began to travel separately in search of food. Then, he had to think for themselves. This was how, gradually, step-by-step, independent mind began to evolve,' said the doctor.

Pandian interrupted, 'It was after that humans began to have individual desires. They began to hoard things for themselves, right Doctor?' he asked.

'Yes. All these are the repercussions of man's evolution. Then, humans split up the whole world into theirs and others,' said the doctor.

'These snow people do not keep anything for themselves,' said Pandian.

'Yes. The reason is they do not have a conscious mind at all. They do not have a sense of self. They only have the subconscious mind,' said the doctor.

'Is that so?' asked Pandian.

'Yes. That evening, Kim went and sat down with them and sang along with them, right? At that time, his subconscious mind merged with their subconsciousness. Immediately, they were able to understand his language too,' the doctor said.

'But we could not mingle with them,' said Pandian.

'Yes. That is why they do not know our language. Snow people are able to talk to all the creatures here without words,' said the doctor.

'How could they do that?' asked Pandian.

'Snow people are able to know all that we think. They then convey it to the bats,' the doctor said.

'That means their mind is connected to the subconscious minds of all the creatures here, right?' Pandian asked.

'Yes. That is the really astonishing fact. While referring to subconscious mind, psychologists refer to human subconsciousness. They do not take into consideration the subconscious minds of animals,' said the doctor.

Just then, Pandian saw something very spectacular. An eagle came flying in from the snow peak in the west. It was an enormous eagle! It was so huge that it covered the western horizon!

'Doctor, what fantastical thing is this?' Pandian exclaimed. That eagle was several kilometres broad. It appeared as if it could lift even big hills in its claws!

When Does a Child Become Aware of Itself?

Psychologists have conducted research on the minds of children. The foremost among them is the scientist Jacques Lacan.

They allege that until 18 months of age, children do not have the sense of "me". Till then, a child identifies itself as a part of other humans and things. That is, if a child sees another child falling, they would cry thinking that they themselves are falling. After 18 months, looking at its hands and legs, a child learns to identify itself. It is only then does it gain the understanding of self.

39

The eagle, which was as vast as the sky, flew fast. Its wings appeared like two dark clouds. Then, it suddenly disappeared.

'Doctor, where did it go?' asked Pandian.

'Wait,' said the doctor. Running his fingers through his hair, he was immersed deep in thought. Then, his face brightened.

'Come, I will show you a wonderful spectacle,' he said.

Immediately, the bats returned to them. They climbed atop the bats and flew towards the snow peak.

'Did not the monstrous eagle fly out from there?' Pandian asked, afraid.

'Do not fear,' reassured the doctor.

They rose in the sky and flew towards the snow peak. The slopes of that snow peak were like the inside of a huge bowl. White snow lay spread over them, making them look like a mirror.

When the bats neared that slope, Pandian saw a wonderous sight. His image was reflected on the mountain, magnified manifold. The image was as huge as a mountain. Pandian understood the phenomenon. That hill was like an enormous concave mirror. If one goes very close to the concave mirror, they will see a massive, virtual image of themself, as if looking through a magnifying glass. When Pandian noticed his hands in the image, they looked like two enormous muddy embankments. The hair on his hands appeared like dark palm trees standing in a line on the banks of a river. Pandian's eyes looked like huge ponds. His eyebrows seemed like elevated banks and his eyelashes appeared to be like palm trees on the banks of that pond. It looked as if the ponds were filled with white water. Pandian realized that it was the image of the whites of his eyes.

A black rock lay at the centre of the white water, and slowly shifted from side to side. Pandian realized that it was the image of his eyeballs. It appeared as if the top part of that rock was embedded with glass. Pandian realized that it was the pupil of his eye.

He saw a small image of himself reflected in that glass. He could see himself flying atop the bat. Pandian stared at his image again. He backed off and glanced at it. Then he neared and took another look. He could not stop his eyes from being fixed on that huge image. There was no other thought in his mind at all. He noticed that his lips appeared like fields of red mud. His nostrils were like two huge caves. His moustache below them was like a thick forest.

Pandian continued to gaze at his image, fascinated.

The doctor called out, 'Pandian! Come, let us go down.'

Pandian did not hear it.

'Pandian, what is this? Let us go down.'

He did not heed it at all.

'Pandian, have you gone mad? Come, let us go down,' shouted the doctor.

Pandian still did not hear anything. He noticed only his image, irrevocably fascinated. How much ever the doctor tried, he could not get Pandian's attention. The doctor's bat swooped down. Standing on the tree's branches, the doctor kept looking worriedly at Pandian. Pandian kept flying in and out, nearing the image and moving back from it. He seemed like a fly hovering over a sweet.

The bat on which Pandian was flying gradually became tired and began to swoop down. Like a paper kite falling, that bat came down. It shrugged Pandian off and he slid down, landing with a thud.

Pandian fell on the tree-top with a bang.

Shocked, he came to his senses.

Immediately, he got up, flustered. He lifted his hands and looked at them. He bent to look at his legs. 'No! This is not me! I am a very big person! I became small when I fell down', Pandian cried in despair.

The doctor hurried towards Pandian, looking at him with concern. 'Pandian, what is all this? What are you gabbling about?'

Pandian blinked like a madman.

'Doctor, my body has become small. I have morphed into an ant!' he cried.

The doctor shook him lightly, calling, 'Pandian, Pandian!'

Pandian immediately jerked awake. He became aware of where he was.

'Your supersized reflection has confused you, Pandian,' said the doctor.

'True. That was a terrible experience!'

'What were you thinking of when you were flying there?'

'I did not think about anything at all, Doctor. My mind was focused on myself, repeating the litany of "Me! Me! Me!"'

'You were hypnotized by that sight. Had the bat not pushed you down, you could have stayed there permanently without even food and water, until you dropped dead.'

'Thanks to my lucky stars I escaped!'

'We spend most of our time thinking only about ourselves,' the doctor said softly.

Pandian felt exhausted. They rested for a while and ate some fruits. Then, they started walking.

At one place, many snow people were romping about. Men, women and children frolicked together in play. That game was like the ones played by very young children. There was no competing in it. Hence, there was no winner or loser either. They were simply gambolling around. They rolled over in somersaults. They shoved at each other. There was joy and fun.

'They spend all their time in play. They do not do anything else,' said the doctor.

Pandian felt a deep yearning. Only when he was a little child had he played happily like this. Then school and studies had taken over his life!

'They do not have any self-awareness. That is why they are so happy,' said the doctor.

They walked deeper into the jungle.

Ice Can Become Lens!

Take clean water in a small bowl. Put that bowl in the fridge. The next day, the water would have frozen into ice. Place the bowl in hot water for a few seconds. Then turn it upside down and tap on it lightly. The ice will come out.

The ice block would be shaped like an idli. We can then use it like a magnifying glass. Objects would be magnified when seen through it. Using that block of ice as a converging lens to focus the sun's rays, even cotton can be set to fire!

40

In the middle of the forest, several snow children were playing. Kim was amid them.

They were playing with a weird creature. It had a trunk while its mouth and face were like that of a lion. Its body was long like a snake's but its legs were like that of a lion. It had small wings too! Flapping its wings, that animal jumped and reached up. It was swinging its trunk playfully.

Pandian recognized that creature immediately.

'Doctor! Do you know what this is? It is *yali*! In the temples back home, this creature would be carved in stone.'

'Ancient animal!'

'But why does it look like a lion?' queried Pandian.

'All the animals here eat only plants. There is no creature here that eats other creatures,' said the doctor.

'You are right. That is why there is no need to fear anything here. Even the mosquitoes here do not bite!' Pandian said.

'In the beginning of evolution, all creatures probably lived like this. Later, when food became scarce, some creatures began to eat other, weaker creatures. For instance, even today, back in our towns, monkeys catch and eat insects when they do not get enough food from plants.'

'But there's no scarcity of food here, right?' asked Pandian.

'I analysed the excretions of all the animals here. All of them pass only dung. They do not pass stool,' said the doctor.

'What is the difference between stool and dung?' asked Pandian.

'The stomachs of animals that eat plants – like, for instance, cows and horses – are different. The food reaches their stomachs and gets mixed up with saliva. There are unique bacteria that live in their stomach that separate the nutrients from food. Those nutrients are absorbed in the intestine, which then sends it to the whole body.'

'How does the digestion happen in other creatures?' asked Pandian.

'For animals – like humans – who eat meat, there are several types of digestive juices that are secreted in their stomach. There are several types of acids in them. Those acids then separate the nutrients from the food,' the doctor explained.

'Is that why our stool smells so bad?'

'Yes. There is no stool here,' said the doctor.

They both lay on their backs, in the sun. Then Kim came and sat near them. He was wearing his clothes now.

The doctor asked, 'What, Kim? You are wearing your clothes again?'

'Let us go back from here, Doctor Saab,' said Kim.

'Why? Have you got bored of this place?' asked the doctor.

'This is Dharmasthala. There is no boredom or sadness here. But we are humans. Lord Buddha has created us in a way that we can live on Earth. We have duties in our world,' said Kim.

The doctor thought for a while. Then he said, 'That is true. Let us leave.'

'I do not have the heart to leave this place at all,' said Pandian.

'Is that even practical? Even if we could spend several years here, we would never be able to finish exploring this forest. Let us leave,' said the doctor.

Pandian got up reluctantly, saying, 'It is enough that we think of leaving. The snow people will come to know if it.'

'Yes. Their permission is necessary for us to leave. Kim, is the work for which you came here over?'

'Why do you ask so?' questioned Kim.

'The snow people wanted us to come here. The reason for it is neither me nor Pandian. I realized it when we reached this place. They wanted you to come here,' said the doctor.

'That is true. Please forgive me. I hid certain things from you,' said Kim.

'I deduced as much! When you saw the snow people, you unhesitatingly went near them and bowed to them. You connected with them easily. This means that when you had been here before, you were fully conscious and aware.'

'You are right. Let me confess everything. In truth, my father did not leave me here by himself.

'Really?' asked Pandian.

'Yes. I was grazing goats in the forest along with my tribe. Then, it seemed as if someone was calling out to us. We followed that voice. That is how we came to the snowy peak. When we reached there, I sensed someone staring intently at me. Immediately my body began to heat up. I got high fever. My father did not know what to do ...'

'What happened then?' Pandian interrupted.

'Then a booming voice was heard from beyond the snow boulders. It ordered that I was to be left behind. My clansmen left me and ran away,' said Kim.

'That is, the yeti planned and brought you here,' said the doctor.

'Yes. On reaching here, they made me sit with them. But I was not able to mingle easily with them. I kept remembering my mother. I kept yearning to go back to my mother. Immediately, they took me back,' said Kim.

'Was it then that Pandian saved you?' asked the doctor.

'Yes. It was only then that I realized that both my parents had abandoned me. They were afraid that their clan would be destroyed if they took me back. For them, their clan was more important than me,' said Kim.

'So, you decided to go back to the snow people, right?' said the doctor.

'Yes, but I would not have been able to come here alone. That is why I joined with you,' said Kim.

'Is your work here finished?' asked the doctor.

'Yes, it is,' said Kim.

'Then, let us start,' said the doctor.

Immediately, three bats came flying.

'The yetis have given their consent. Let us go,' said Kim.

According to Indian Rishis, There Are Four Minds!

Freud discovered the existence of only three types of minds. But 2,000 years before that, Indian sages discovered that there are four types of minds.

The wise Indian sages refer to the surface conscious mind as *jagrat*. They call the subconscious mind *swapnan*. The unconscious mind is called *sukshubdhi*. The fourth mind is even deeper and vast. Its name is *thuriyam*. This encompasses the minds of all beings including animals, birds and insects. Buddhists refer to thuriyam as the 'science of temple'.

41

Kim gave some seeds to Pandian and the doctor. They looked like almonds. 'These are the seeds of a really rare medicinal herb that grows here. If you eat them, you will feel neither hungry nor thirsty. All types of nutrients are packed in these medicinal seeds.'

Pandian and the doctor put the seeds in their mouths and chewed on them. They tasted like peppermint toffees.

Kim had a small bag with him. He had collected several seeds of medicinal plants in it. 'There are enough seeds in here for us to eat till we reach our place,' said Kim.

Pandian ran and fetched a box.

'Where did you find this?' asked the doctor. 'Is this not the box that we lost in the river?'

'Yes. I found this at the riverbank,' said Pandian.

'What is there in this?' asked the doctor.

'All the things that I gathered here – insects, flowers, stones, leaves all are inside,' said Pandian.

They climbed on the bats. They rose, flying into the sky.

'Do we not have to take leave from the yetis?' asked Pandian.

'They know how to send us off,' said Kim.

They rose in the sky. On the mirror-like surface of the snow mountain opposite, a snowman's face could be seen, magnified manifold. His eyes were like two blue pools. He bid them farewell with his eyes. Another face could be seen on another mountain slope. Their visages bid farewell to the three. The angle of their vision differed as they flew. Depending on that, the faces of different snow people could be seen reflected on those mountain slopes. It appeared as if the mountains themselves sprouted faces and bid them farewell. After they had crossed the frozen sea, the bats landed on the ground. The three of them alighted and the bats flew back.

'I feel as if I have woken up from a dream,' said Pandian.

'Yes. What a wonderful dream! What a magnificent dream!' said the doctor.

'Dreams do not come from outside. They are within us,' said Kim.

'You declared that the purpose for which you had come was fulfilled. Could you please tell me what that purpose was?' asked Pandian.

'I cannot explain it easily. I achieved the greatest enlightenment that could possibly be achieved by any human,' said Kim.

The doctor said, 'I do not understand.'

'There are three stages in meditation. The first stage is the conscious stage. The second stage is referred to as the dream-like state. The third stage is the deep-sleep stage,' said Kim.

'Is that so?' said Pandian.

'There is a stage beyond these three. That is the pinnacle of mediation. It is called thuriya stage.'

'How will that be?' asked the doctor.

'It will be difficult to explain it using words. At that stage, we do not understand ourselves as a separate entity. There would not be a feeling of 'I' at all. It is the stage where all the living beings of Earth are united. Worms, insects, animals , birds, humans, all become one. Then, there will be only one collective mind. It is a mind with neither a beginning nor an end. We would be merged with that.'

'What would happen if a raindrop fell into the sea? This is similar to that, right?' asked the doctor.

'Yes,' said Kim.

'Did you reach that stage here?' asked Pandian.

'Yes. One can achieve that stage only if one meditates for several long years. Then, too, such a stage will last only a little while. But after coming here, I was completely in such a state. I came out of it only when I spoke with you in the middle of it.'

'Who are you?' asked Pandian.

'I am the Buddha. But each and every worm on this

Earth is the same as me. Even a small virus is on par with me,' said Kim.

'I do not understand,' said Pandian.

'It cannot be understood that easily,' said Kim.

'What is this foul smell?' asked the doctor suddenly.

'Foul smell?' questioned Pandian.

'Yes. As if something had rotted,' said the doctor.

'Yes. Something smells bad,' agreed Pandian. Immediately he had a suspicion. He opened his bag and looked inside it. The different varieties of plants and flowers he had gathered in it had begun to rot.

'Aha! Everything has rotted,' exclaimed Pandian.

'How can those survive here? They grow there in a different temperature and environment, don't they?' said the doctor.

They were walking on the snowy expanse. Pandian was throwing down the rotten plants from his bag. There was just one flower that was not rotten. He gave it in Kim's hands and turned his bag upside down.

'I had collected all these as memories of our journey here,' said Pandian.

'Let it be! At least you are left with one flower,' said the doctor.

Then, two Buddhist monks came running from beyond the little snowy hillock opposite them.

'Bodhisattva! Bodhisattva Padmapani!' one of them proclaimed.

'Maha Lama! Maha Lama!' the other monk declared.

Pandian turned around in surprise. There was a golden-coloured lotus in Kim's hands.

It was the same flower that Pandian had taken from his bag a little while ago.

That lotus shone brightly, as if it were made of gold. It was because he had seen many wondrous things there, that Pandian had not paid much attention to it. It was one of the flowers that he had stuffed into his bag in his hurry to leave. The two monks were the ones they had seen before. They came running and fell to their knees at Kim's feet.

'Bodhisattva Padmapani! The Buddha holding the golden lotus! You are our Maha Lama!' they said.

'It is my duty,' Kim said softly.

The monk chanted, '*Buddham saranam gachami! Dharmam saranam gachami! Sangam saranam gachami!*'

Kim too chanted after them.

Immediately, one monk opened his cloth bundle. He took out a golden crown from inside. It was the crown worn by the lamas. It was studded with several priceless diamonds and rubies. It was radiantly luminous.

'Maha Lama should accompany us to our monastery. You must take your seat as our guru,' said one monk.

'The Buddha has assigned me that duty,' said Kim.

The doctor fell at Kim's feet and venerated him. 'Maha Lama! Please bless me,' he said.

'The blessings of Lord Buddha are always with you.'

Pandian too clasped his palms together in respect. He was taken aback to see the doctor bowing and falling at the feet of the boy.

Kim addressed Pandian, saying, 'We will meet again!'

Then he turned back and began to walk. The monks followed him.

Collective Consciousness

Carl Gustav Jung was one of the important psychiatrists of the twentieth century.

He proved how everyone's unconscious mind is related to that of the others. He referred to this as collective unconscious.

For millions of years, billions of humans have been born; they have lived and died. But their unconscious mind does not die at all. It merges with the other unconscious minds.

Let us assume that a river keeps flowing. But the shadow that falls on the water remains unchanged, does it not? This is similar to that!

42

Pandian and the doctor continued to walk.

'Now, we have to find our way ourselves. We have to be very careful,' said the doctor.

Pandian asked, 'Doctor, why did you venerate Kim by falling at his feet?'

'Is he not the Maha Lama?' said the doctor.

'Is he not just an ordinary tribal boy from the mountains? And you are such a highly educated person!' asked Pandian.

'Wisdom does not come from just being educated. Only when we apply that knowledge into our lives do we become wise. Wisdom is the most vital thing. If intelligence is not guided, it becomes worthless. That is why an enlightened person is far superior to the greatest intellectual.'

'How to recognize enlightened people?'

'Enlightened people are the ones who have attained maturity of the mind. They do not have the feeling of "I" and "me". Hence, they will not be materialistic. As they are not selfish, they will not keep anything for themselves. Because they do not hoard, they will not be afraid of others. So, they will not get jealous or angry. They will not be sad when they lose anything. That is, someone who is always in a calm state of mind is an enlightened person,' said the doctor.

'Did they not place a crown made of diamonds on Kim's head?' queried Pandian.

'Yes. Possessions should be held by the person who does not have any attachments. Even fame should lie with the person does not have the least desire for it,' replied the doctor.

Suddenly, Pandian realized that he had lost his way. 'Doctor, we have lost our way.'

'This is not the way we first went there. The bats have dropped us at some other place. There must be some reason for it. I am calmly observing everything, and trying to understand why,' said the doctor.

They kept walking on the snow. Pandian did not feel tired at all. How much ever far he walked, he did not feel breathless; nor did his legs pain. The wound on his hands had completely healed. There was not even a tiny scar there.

When they reached the edge of a peak, the doctor pointed, 'Look there!'

There was a big pedestal there. It was covered with snow.

'What is that pedestal?' asked Pandian.

'Let us see,' said the doctor. They both neared it. The doctor climbed atop it and looked around on all four sides and said, 'Aha!'

'What, Doctor?' asked Pandian.

'Look there.'

Pandian looked at the direction the doctor pointed. There was a big mountain in that direction and they could see a very remarkable scene. At first, Pandian did not understand what was going on. It appeared to be just a green-coloured reflection. Then he realized what it was.

It was the forest where the snow people lived. The reflection of that forest could be seen inverted on the curved face of that snow mountain.

'In a concave mirror, far off images get inverted,' said the doctor.

He carefully observed the image of that forest. He was able to recognize the places they had been to. The snow people were frolicking about. Different varieties of peculiar birds flew above. Unusual creatures roamed about. Pandian felt a deep yearning. When he had been there, he had not felt despair, even for a second. He had only felt joy there. Pandian questioned if he could ever go back there. Suddenly, he felt an urge to cry.

'This pedestal was built by humans. We can pay respects to the forest where the snow people live. There must be someone who comes here and venerates the snow people thus,' said the doctor.

'It must be the monks who pray to them,' said Pandian.

'If it is so, then there must be some place near here where the monks live,' he said.

'Let us explore,' said Pandian.

They scanned that region. There was no building to be seen anywhere. Suddenly, the doctor said, 'Pandian, do you notice the snow-covered boulder over there?'

A finial could be seen on the top of the boulder – similar to the ones placed at the topmost tips of temple towers. But it was covered with snow.

'This means the temple has been covered by snow,' said Pandian.

They both neared that rock. It was covered with snow on all sides.

'Is there a temple inside this? If so, where is its entrance?' asked Pandian.

'Look here. There are tiny air bubbles in the snow. It means that the entrance is here. This is the air that comes from inside,' said the doctor.

Pandian knocked hard at the snow with his hand. The snow broke and shattered like glass.

It was the entrance of that monastery. There were no doors, only steps made of stone.

They climbed on those steps and reached a big room. That room was perfectly circular in shape. Its roof looked like an upturned bowl. From somewhere, soft light entered the room. A gentle breeze blew in too. Pandian deduced that there must be small air-holes somewhere. When air blew in through them, the soft sounds of flute could be heard.

'What an amazing place of worship!' Pandian exclaimed in wonder. 'This monastery is made by hollowing out natural rock. I have seen such cave temples in Ajanta too!'

'Yes. It must be several years since this was built,' said the doctor.

The walls of that circular room were curved. There were a large number of sculptures in the room.

'These are all the images of Bodhisattva. There are many such Bodhisattvas,' explained the doctor.

'Who are Bodhisattvas?' asked Pandian.

'They who attain the pinnacle of enlightenment according to the path shown by Lord Buddha are the Bodhisattvas. Wait, there is something written here,'The doctor read the words written in the Tibetan language. 'Pandian do you know what is this? This is the temple for the Buddha Maitreyar. They have built this to welcome him when He arrives,' said the doctor.

'How will Maitreyar arrive here?' asked Pandian.

'Look how they have built this monastery. This is open towards the area where the snow people are living,' said the doctor.

'If that is so, will the Maitreyar come from there?' asked Pandian.

'That is what the people who built this had believed,' said the doctor.

They walked around, looking at the walls. 'Look at these sculptures! All the animals that we saw in the snow people's place are represented here!' exclaimed Pandian.

Just then, they heard the sound of a door opening near them. The doctor and Pandian turned around in panic.

A door made of stone moved and opened. A doorway could be seen. A monk came out of it. On seeing him, the doctor and Pandian were shocked.

He was very old. His body was withered and dry. His skin was wrinkled like a dried banana sheath. There was no hair on his head or face. His eyes were sunken into their sockets. His body trembled as he walked.

'Who are you?' asked the doctor.

'My name is Dorje Samyakpa! I am the four hundred and twentieth Maha Lama of the Siva-o-Repa monastery. I have been living here for the last hundred years,' said the old man.

Cave Temples

There is a place called Ajanta in the state of Maharashtra. Huge Buddhist monasteries have been built there by hollowing out the rocks.

Mahayana Buddhists built Ajanta. There are incredible paintings in the walls of those caves.

The uniqueness of these structures lies in the fact that the statue of the Buddha in the sanctum, the walls of the temple and the steps are all made of a single rock.

43

Pandian asked incredulously, 'For a hundred years? How old are you?'

'I am two hundred and fifty years old. The head lamas of the Siva-o-Repa monastery all live for one hundred and fifty years,' said the lama.

The doctor said, 'The new head lama of the Siva-o-Repa monastery was escorted there just today.'

'I am aware of that. This is him, right?' saying so, the lama pointed at the wall.

There was a statue of Kim on the wall. He was standing with a diamond crown on his head, holding a golden lotus in his hands. Next to it was a statue of Kim as he would become when he grew old.

'Once Bodhisattva Padmapani reaches Tibet, the previous Maha Lama will come here. I will renounce this place to him and go to Dharmasthala,' said the Maha Lama.

'Why are you living here? Are there no other human beings here at all?' asked Pandian.

'I am the priest of Buddha Maitreyar. This is the temple of Buddha Maitreyar. For the past three thousand years, this practice has been going on,' said the lama.

The doctor and Pandian venerated the lama by falling at his feet. He blessed them both.

'You can come to my room and rest awhile,' the lama invited.

That room was small in size. The skin of a woolly mammoth was spread on the floor there. It was cosy and warm there. 'I do not eat any food. I just eat a type of seed from Dharmasthala. One seed is enough for a day,' said the lama.

'We have that seed with us too,' said the doctor.

'How?'

The doctor described in detail their journey into the snow people's forest.

'You must be really blessed to meet the yetis,' said the lama.

'Why has this temple been built facing Dharmasthala?' asked the doctor.

'Because Maitreyar Buddha will come from there,' said the lama.

'Why?' asked the doctor.

'*Maitreyi* means unity. *Maitreya* means the embodiment of oneness. Maitreya means not differentiating between I, you, this, that in this world. The yetis live in that state,' the lama said.

'Why are they like that?' mused Pandian.

'They have monkey's hands. Their hands have not evolved,' said the doctor.

'That is exactly the reason! They do not perform any action. Hence their hands have not evolved.'

'Why do they not do any action?' asked Pandian.

'Because they do not see things separate from themselves. They do not have the feeling of "I". Hence, they have no need for houses and clothes. They live connected with nature.'

'We live competing with nature. We create luxuries for ourselves like houses and clothes,' said the doctor.

'Yes. We call such actions as *karmam*. The word *karam** has evolved from the word karmam. The yetis' karmam has not evolved. Hence wisdom grew. As we focused on karmam, our wisdom did not evolve,' said the lama.

Pandian recollected what the doctor had explained. It is the forebrain that controls language and hands. In the snow people's brain, the part that relates to the hands has not developed. Compensating for that, the part that relates to language has developed better.

The Maha Lama said, 'Do pray to Maitreyar Buddha before you leave!'

They came to the main hall of the monastery again. The sanctum was at the far end of the main hall. Pandian and the doctor followed the lama there.

---

* Karam means hands in Tamil.

The sanctum was very dark. When they looked inside keenly, they could see a big statue of Lord Buddha inside. It was a statue of the Buddha in meditation. The lama stood at a particular place and looked up. 'Saranam! Saranam!' he cried.

Immediately its sound echoed from the roof of that sanctum. Due to the vibration produced by that echo, the sound of some far-off glacier splitting was heard. Then, the sound of that glacier breaking and falling down was heard. It fell on a huge bell. Immediately a loud ringing sound was heard. Light spread inside the sanctum too.

Pandian was stunned when he saw the statue of the Buddha inside.

It was the Snowman! The Buddha's statue was in the image of the Snowman. Its fingers and toes were like that of a monkey. On the head of that statue, there was a pale, red-coloured crown. The crown gradually began to shine with the reflected light. It was only then that Pandian realized that the crown was a flawless diamond. That diamond was like a snow crystal.

The statue of the Buddha, which was in the image of the Snowman, had two blue-coloured diamonds for its eyes. They were the exact shade of the Snowman's eyes. It seemed as if Maitreyar Buddha was looking at them keenly.

The doctor and Pandian bowed to Maitreyar Buddha.

The lama sang a song in Tibetan:

Oh Buddha
The very form of Dharma
I salute you!
You are the one
Who cannot be secerned into
Yesterday, today and tomorrow.
You are the One-
Undifferentiated between I, you, that, this
Unbound by karma
Wisdom incarnate
Without sorrows
Without any evil
Interfused with trees, plants, grass, rotts, worms,
insects, germs, birds, animals
Inseparably one with everything
Embodiment of Benevolence!
Maitreyar Buddha!
A thousand times I bow to you.

Then, Pandian and the doctor took leave from the lama. The lama guided them in the right direction.

'We will go back in a few days,' said the doctor.

'Yes. Once they receive my report, the entire government will be shaken. The world will be stupefied. Television cameras will pile up in that forest. Scientists and researchers will gather there,' said Pandian.

'It is exactly about this that I want to discuss with you, Pandian. Do we really need to reveal this?' asked the doctor.

'What are you saying, Doctor? We have reached here after so many struggles. What an astonishing discovery we have made! Why should we not discuss this outside?' asked Pandian.

An Amazing Organ

Among all the organs in the human body, which is that one part that has evolved far beyond that of any other animal?

It is our thumb!

Our thumb is necessary for our hands to perform all actions. We would be amazed when we think of all the different types of activities our thumb would perform in a day. The thumb is very strong too. In the course of evolution, as humans continuously used their hands, the thumb evolved thus!

44

'Do you know what will happen once you submit your report?' asked the doctor.

'What will happen?' asked Pandian.

'The Indian Army will take control of the forest. It will claim all the resources in there for itself.'

'But that region is spread over China and India.'

'Yes. Immediately, China will declare war. Thousands of people will die in such a war. The entire forest might get destroyed with a single bomb. Atomic bombs might be deployed too. Then the world will be destroyed,' said the doctor.

'This is all mere speculation. Why can't India and China agree to share the forest equally?' asked Pandian.

'What you are saying now is speculation. Has something like that happened anywhere in this world? How many wars have been fought for resources? How many millions of people were killed? Just think,' said the doctor.

'Is this not incredible news, Doctor? How can we keep this a secret?' asked Pandian.

'How many such incredible forests were there on this Earth! The Amazon Rainforest is a hundred times bigger than this one. Today two-thirds of it has been destroyed.'

'Do you think humans would destroy this forest too?' asked Pandian.

'Definitely. Because humans are full of avarice. They strive to make everything their own. They would strive to use everything for themselves. They will mercilessly destroy the things that are not useful to them,' said the doctor.

'Humans aren't such cruel creatures, Doctor.'

'Yes! Humans aren't ruthless. How many elephants lived in the forests of our country? How many tigers? We destroyed many of them. In some years, they might become extinct too. Do you know how many species have been completely destroyed? For humans, the top priority is their wants and needs. They will do anything to satisfy them,' said the doctor.

Pandian had no reply.

'If information about the existence of these forests is known outside, immediately business-minded people will gather here. They would capture the rare creatures, put them in cages and train them to perform acts of entertainment. They would kill off all the animals that can't be trained. They will sell their skin and meat. Not only animals, they would not even leave the trees alone. Why, humans would even sell the stones and soil there.'

'I am not able to accept what you say,' said Pandian.

'This is what human history teaches us. Even a hundred years ago, the African continent was as flourishing and rich as these forests. The people there lived happily. Today, all of Africa's forests have been destroyed and the continent has become like a desert. A severe famine occurred there. Millions of people are dying there due to lack of food. Humankind has looted most of Earth. Pandian, only certain rare places are left intact.'

'Can't I just inform only our scientists about these forests?' asked Pandian.

'For what purpose do the scientists conduct research? It is only for the benefit of humankind, right? They would think from the perspective of what discoveries would profit humans. Do you know what these researchers would do? They would capture the snow people and put them in cages! They would give them several types of medicines and perform experiments on them. They would think about whether snow people could be trained and made into slaves to serve humans. Do you know what happened to the African apes? Scientists from the European countries captured and used them for their experiments. They conducted several experiments and tortured the innocent animals. Are you aware that apes like gorillas, chimpanzees and orangutans are endangered and would be extinct soon?'

The doctor ran out of breath and panted after his long, passionate speech.

'Is there no one among humans who is merciful and kind?' asked Pandian.

'Yes. There are. Individually, men have mercy. But humankind has no mercy at all. Because the human lifestyle is such. Human culture is thus. They can live only by destroying nature. They have become used to it,' the doctor said.

'Do I not have to perform my duty?' asked Pandian.

'Is your responsibility towards your job more important than the future of this Earth?' asked the doctor angrily.

'Doctor, I am a military man. My duty ...'

The doctor quickly countered him. 'What duty? Is it your duty to destroy this wonderful forest? Is it your duty to endanger the snow people, who are frolicking about like little children, put them in cages and torture them?'

The doctor's eyes welled up. Pandian teared up too. In defence research laboratories, he had seen several types of monkeys. To understand how poisons and viruses work, their bodies would be injected with the chemicals and microbes. He had even seen many monkeys suffer and die a painful death. Those researchers would similarly put the snow people in cages and conduct such experiments on them. The snow people's beautiful blue eyes flashed in his mind.

'No, Doctor! No! I will submit a report that the Snowman is a mere figment of imagination,' Pandian cried.

The doctor let out a big sigh of relief. Then he said, 'The snow people have to live, Pandian.'

'Why?' asked Pandian.

'Two types of human species evolved from *Ramapithecus* monkeys. One is us. The other is the snow people. Both are two different types of evolution. Our hands evolved. Their intellect evolved. We developed by fighting against nature. They developed by living symbiotically with nature. Which is the correct path?' asked the doctor.

'I do not know,' admitted Pandian.

'Today our human civilization has attained a high stage of development. We have even reached the moon. But we have not attained wisdom. On one side, millions of people go hungry. On the other, so many people live in the lap of luxury. Humans make other humans their slaves. For the sake of wealth, they wage wars against each other and die,' said the doctor.

'Yes, Doctor. After seeing the snow people, I have begun to hate the life led by humans. Isn't our life filled with jealousy, greed and grief?' said Pandian.

'Humans have destroyed nature. There is only very little nature left on this Earth. The human population is increasing. At some point, we could reach a stage where humans can no longer live on Earth. Famine and disease might occur on a global scale. Immediately, many wars might take place. Then, the human race itself might become extinct.'

'You are right, Doctor.'

'Those monks were right. They said that the snow people were like grains of seed. It is true. If the human race becomes extinct, then perhaps the snow people will spread and populate this Earth! They live along with nature. They will adapt themselves according to nature. Therefore, they will not become extinct,' said the doctor.

'Yes, Doctor. That is true.'

'Since three thousand years, the Tibetan Buddhists have known about the snow people. But they did not reveal this secret at all. This is the reason for that. In the course of evolution, among two alternative paths, if one fails, the other has a chance at success, right? It is highly essential that the snow people are left alive on this Earth. When the human race becomes extinct, they would spread all over Earth. A new civilization will be created on this Earth.'

Pandian said, 'You are right doctor. We saw with our own eyes what such a civilization would be like.'

The doctor turned and looked at the snowy mountains. Light fell on his face, illuminating it. He said in a passionate voice, 'It would be a civilization that does not destroy nature! Humans, too, would live as a part of nature. There will not be a feeling of "I" there. Nobody will have any possessions there. So, everybody would be equal and everyone will live in unity!'

The doctor spread out his hands. He said in an exalted tone, 'A world without partitions! A world without diseases and war! A world without grief! A golden world filled only with joy! *Kiruthayugam!* Let Kiruthayugam come! Let Kiruthayugam arrive! May Maitreya Buddha be born!' His voice echoed in the mountains.

Tears flowed from Pandian's eyes. He ran towards the doctor and hugged him.

'We are indeed lucky people, Pandian. We are returning after seeing a great existential truth,' said the doctor.

'Yes,' said Pandian. He then took out a small parcel from his pocket and threw it away.

'What was it?' asked the doctor.

'A diamond! I had kept it secretly. Only now do I realize what a shameful action that was. I am a soldier. It is only bravery that gives me joy. What need do I have for this diamond and the wealth from it?' said Pandian.

'Are we not mere human beings? I too had the same desire. I had also pocketed some diamond stones. I threw them away when I saw the Maha Lama for the first time,' said the doctor.

'You mean Kim?' asked Pandian.

'Yes. He did not covet anything even for an instant. He is wise by nature,' said the doctor.

Pandian immediately realized everything. 'Yes, Doctor. I now understand clearly. What a big blunder I had made. I got a chance to meet a Maha Lama and spend time with him. Despite that, I did not pay any obeisance or get blessings from him,' said Pandian.

'Do not worry. The Maha Lama took leave of me directly. But he told you that you will meet again. You will surely meet him again,' said the doctor.

'Where? When? How?' asked Pandian.

'That is in the future. We cannot see it. Only enlightened people can see the future,' said the doctor.

They climbed down the snowy expanse.

'Please check the route carefully, Doctor,' said Pandian.

'We do not have to worry at all. We will not face any danger. We will not lose our way, either. We have sentinels guarding us,' said the doctor.

'Sentinels?' asked Pandian.

'Yes. Look over there,' pointed the doctor.

Pandian looked at where the doctor pointed. A huge footprint of the Snowman was on the ground! The doctor and Pandian paid respects to the Snowman in their hearts. Then they began to descend from the mountains.

How Do Civilizations Become Extinct?

You might have heard of the Sumerian civilization. There was a place called Mesopotamia in today's Iraq. It lay between two rivers called Euphrates and Tigris. It was here that the Sumerian civilization flourished.

How did that civilization end? The Sumerians built dams to store the waters of Euphrates and Tigris rivers. They farmed their lands, irrigating them with that water. That region has a very hot climate. High amounts of water will become water vapour. The salts and sediments in the water alone will remain in the soil. Like this, the agricultural lands in Mesopotamia became barren saline lands.

Then, the Sumerians left those lands and farmed other lands. They, too, turned barren. There was no land left for agriculture. Due to lack of food, severe famines affected Mesopotamia. Gradually the Sumerian civilization vanished. Now that area is a desert.

In this world, there were many civilizations like this. All those civilizations steadily died as they destroyed nature.

Acknowledgements

Heartfelt thanks to Jeyamohan Sir for his trust and support.

Thanks to my parents and grandparents for surrounding me with books from a young age and inculcating the habit of reading in me; my husband for his complete faith in me, which gave me the confidence to take up this project; and my boisterous and talkative children who gave me the space when I needed it the most.

Gratitude to my best friends Rupasree and Kavitha, my ardent cheerleaders who are always there for me.

Thanks to my beta reader Dhivya Balaji for her insightful comments and keen interest in this project.

Many thanks to stalwarts Arunava Sinha, Jerry Pinto and Tejaswini Niranjana, whose seminars and workshops gave me the necessary tools and confidence in my translation journey.

I am grateful to my tribe of fellow translators and friends Purnima, Shraddha, Subhashri, Arpita, Suchitra, Aishwarya and Radhika for their conversations and camaraderie. Special thanks to Priyamvada for being the trailblazer in taking Tamil translations to the international stage.

Thanks to the illustrator Shanmugavel Velu and cover designers Gavin Morris and Bhanu Pratap for their eye-catching work.

I am thankful to Chiki Sarkar for her confidence in this translation and the team at Juggernaut – Smita Mathur and Ayushi Choudhary – for their meticulous editing and diligent fact-checking.

Thanks to Kanishka Gupta for taking this book to the right place.

A special shout out to Padmapriya L.D., Saatvik Srivatsan, Srikrithi M., Aravindh V., Saadana Anugrahaa K.S., Tanushri M., Camillus Nihal Raj and Varnika A. – students of Budding Minds International School, Manimangalam, Chennai, who, along with the guidance of their teacher C. Annapoorani, have also translated this story. Though I have not had the pleasure of reading that translation, their interest and commitment cemented my faith on the universality and timelessness of this book.

Notes on the Author and Translator

B. Jeyamohan (b. 1962), based in Nagercoil, Tamil Nadu, is a pre-eminent writer in modern Tamil literature. Apart from his other landmark novels such as *Vishnupuram* (1997) and *Kotravai* (2005), his body of work includes more than three hundred short stories, many volumes of literary criticism, biographies, travelogues, introductory texts to Indian and Western literature as well as essays on heritage and philosophy. He won the Akilan Memorial Prize for his first novel, and the Katha Samman and the Sanskriti Samman awards.

V. Shyamala is a chartered global management accountant and content specialist who loves to read. When she became a mother of two bookworms, she started a joyous treasure hunt for books to feed their insatiable appetites. Along the way, she discovered her passion for finding and translating children's books from Tamil into English so that even more bookworms hop on for the fun ride!